Caroline Hagood

GOBLIN MODE

A Speculative
Memoir

sfwp.com

Library of Congress Cataloging-in-Publication Data pending

Names: Hagood, Caroline author
Title: Goblin mode : a speculative memoir / Caroline Hagood.
Description: Santa Fe, NM: SFWP, 2025. | Summary: "In Caroline Hagood's
    GOBLIN MODE, the protagonist, who is and is not Caroline Hagood, takes a
    surreal odyssey through humor, horror, and plague-time Brooklyn. In a
    supercharged three-day stretch, she navigates a city full of flashers
    and parrots who talk to her on subways, makes an ominous visit to a
    bioluminescent bay in Fajardo, Puerto Rico at Christmastime, mothers two
    spirited children in an apartment that's probably haunted, and lives in
    a world that may or may not be about to shut down. This state of goblin
    mode that she inhabits is metaphorical, said to have taken root since
    Covid and all the other sociopolitical unrest. But it's also very real,
    in the form of an actual goblin that has been following her around since
    childhood, daring her to live more fiercely..."—Provided by publisher.
Identifiers: LCCN 2024049635 | ISBN 9781951631499 paperback |
    · ISBN 9781951631505 ebook
Subjects: LCSH: Hagood, Caroline—Fiction | LCGFT: Autobiographical fiction |
    Fantasy fiction | Novels
Classification: LCC PS3608.A378 G63 2025 | DDC 813/.6—dc23/eng/20250304
LC record available at https://lccn.loc.gov/2024049635

Published by SFWP
369 Montezuma Ave. #350
Santa Fe, NM 87501
www.sfwp.com

I want it to be beautiful, even when the subject is hard.
Honey, the question is, how do you want to exist in the world,
and how are you going to do the work?
—Nick Cave

I just feel that we, as a society, would not allow a woman
to express her rich-enough inner life by writing down every
single thing she does and putting it into a book.
—Carmen Maria Machado

I walked around all morning receiving ideas from the city.
—Jami Attenberg

But it matters, how we assemble things,
how we put things together.
—Sara Ahmed

For Max, Layla, and Adriel

For my family

For my friends

For my students

For my professor friend of the fries and good diner coffee

For my coffee cart guy

Contents

1. Stay Tuned

I wake early each morning, before the kids, to write and see the real city—my Brooklyn curving in on itself, the prose poem of citywide snow removal and garbage pick-ups, but also geese migrating over Kings County rooftops in V-formation. Even the concept of oversleeping has become specious to me because it implies there's a right time to rise. I press snooze: an act of rebellion most likely related to a middle age with the tags still on. Inhabitant of an apartment that's probably haunted, mother of two, obsessive voyager of my plague-time city, tiny space sojourner riding a decaying world and body to the end of the line. This week I'm ready to change everything, though, or more likely to crack in half. The question remains: what stunning new-fangled creature will crawl out of me when I do? Stay tuned.

There's no rising before the kids to write or track geese this morning, though. Instead, the day starts when tiny fingers brush my face as I feel my six-year-old daughter sitting on my head while her nine-year-old brother screams from the other room that his head is stuck in the laundry basket again. This happens when he pretends to be "Boxhead" to make us laugh. It truly is hilarious. So, we always laugh. And then he does it again. But it's not as funny so early in the morning.

She whispers a confession, her hot little-girl-breath in my ear, that she's actually a unicorn and is that okay? I nod, my eyes still glued shut, as she starts to rattle off everyone in her class's favorite snack foods, who's allergic to peanuts, and the exact kind of unicorn she wants to attend her roller-skating birthday party, which we've never discussed, almost a year from now. Eyes still closed, I can see in high-definition her future operatic disappointment at her party when no unicorn is in attendance. I put this on my mental thousand-page-long to-fix-in-the-future list.

I remove my daughter from my head, screw open my eyes to see the tail-end of her as she dashes off. I follow to find that my son's just joking, as he runs around the room with the laundry basket on his head, but not stuck there. I take the basket off his head, and he runs into my room. I enter to find him leaving a note on my pillow. Now the girl's banging on the drums I'd given her without really thinking it through as I pick up the note my son has left.

2. Someday We're All Going to Die

The note says, with my son's signature dark sense of humor, *someday we're all going to die*. I just want to tell you that my friends without kids sleep in. They do things like go to Paris, France. Nobody leaves them creepy pillow notes or sits on their heads unless they ask them to. They don't need to wipe anyone else's behind.

The sun has not yet fully risen, and my son breaks a vase while trying to use it as a microphone. Then, as I'm taking out the trash with the shattered vase in it, a raccoon jumps out of the garbage can with a piece of pizza in its mouth, and now I think today's the day to tell my story.

The humor, the horror, the wonder. How to chronicle it all? I can't, but what I can do is lie on my back in bed after the pizza-raccoon incident, craving pizza, still in my pajamas. My heart beating so hard it causes my eyes to palpitate. Tuning my vision to a one-two rhythm. Transforming the visual into a tactile register. A region of touch. Right now, I'm using the voice record function and something about speaking instead of writing makes me feel like this doesn't have to fit anyone's idea of what a book should be.

I suppose I should start at the beginning. But when, in writing, have I ever done what I was supposed to do? Let's put it this way: one day this goblin came to me and said, *write straight from your body—just open your skin and pour what comes out onto the page—blood, guts, what have you.* I took it a step further, though, and invited you in. It was so sexy.

In this speculative take on what writing could be, I skip over the translation step, give you a direct tour of my thinking tubes. For each one I provide the tale of how it got to be that way. The ducts are slick, and you slide down easily. If you're bored with my inner life, you don't show it, and I love you for it in a way that borders on illegal.

3. Let's Keep it Dangerous

L et's keep it dangerous since we both know I'm a pervert when it comes to matters of the intellect. I just sit around all day like: *how can I put my mind around that place where thought emerges?* Then I try to write about it. I don't feel like it's actual writing unless I burn out my computer, smoke puffing from its mechanical gills, in the same liminal state of system overdrive I find myself in daily. So here I lie, under my smoking MacBook Air, creative deviant, a woman with a story to tell.

My son reappears in the room. He wants to know if we can go to Coney Island after school to do the haunted house ride. It's our favorite. We squeal during the newish part where they spritz you with a liquid that's meant to feel like blood. Then we go put on 3D glasses and shoot up the monsters taking over New York City in the virtual reality game nearby. Pictures of who's ahead in the game flash onscreen while you play. I always get way too into it, and we giggle as a ferocious image of me pops up, holding a laser gun, a post-apocalyptic road warrior. Sounds about right. I tell him Deno's Wonder Wheel Amusement Park isn't open in cold weather and he slinks off looking sadder than anyone ever. I yell after him that I can make zombie pancakes this morning, hoping it will be a close second, but he tells me it's too late for zombie pancakes. It's five antemeridian.

Note I scribbled myself on the first draft of this creature. Don't worry about what this is: kill genre. Let this book be the creeping vine that can't seem to stay in the garden. Even if it turns you into a goblin. Whether I can deliver on this remains to be seen. But what if I were to use it as a verb and start to goblin around? What would that even look like? Let's find out.

When *Oxford Dictionaries* selected "goblin mode" as its 2022 plague-time term of the year, the president of Oxford Languages noted the role language plays in processing our experiences. Naming the surrealist experiment of their post-pandemic lives helped people identify and cope with it. He concluded that during the pandemic, folks were getting in touch with their inner goblins.

In quarantine, we discovered we'd made the imagined thoughts practical strangers had about us more real than anything we thought. But then these practical strangers were reduced to talking heads on videotelephony software, and we got that their opinions had been virtual all along. We had no way of knowing what they thought about us one way or the other, and yet we always assumed the worst, and let this curb what we did with our single electric life. The charged, symbolic creature roaring at the center of *Goblin Mode* was our lucky portal to that very electricity.

When Governor Cuomo placed New York City, then the Corona epicenter, on pause on March 20, 2020, it was a time of doing laps in bedsheet candy wrappers, letting pizza boxes become our new homes, discovering unseen patterns on ceilings, our greasy hair forming a sad kind of halo; but it was also a time of letting go of so many things we did to please others, and trying to figure out, by trawling our own subterranean expanses, what truly pleased us. In many cases, this involved choosing creativity over capitalism, dirty over clean, experimentation over conformity, the curation of chaos over any attempt at order.

Not that anybody needs to be a goblin scholar (I'm sure not one), but the articles on goblin mode played up laziness and greed and ignored the creativity involved in the goblinesque rejection of societal rules. Goblins are shapeshifters, tricksters, agents of invention and change, anger and anarchy, demons doing away with the old ways, and therefore also about innovation. And if there's anything the world needed in 2022, it was a good old-fashioned goblin transformation trick. I certainly did.

In every photo, standing behind me is my braver, more inventive goblin self who takes nonsense from no one. I call her…Goblin. I later learn the word for a woman goblin is goblette. She peers out from the photograph that encloses her, impatient, waiting for me to make mischief, but I'm too busy cleaning up crumbs and ensuring nobody in the galaxy has any unmet needs. I recognize her. She's been around since childhood, trying to transform me into something fiercer.

So, how about I give you the structure of this fabulist beast upfront as a sort of warning? Hello, this will be a memoir with lies, a novel with truth. A movel? Welcome, I'm very glad to have you here. Feel free to leave your shoes on. It's not that kind of home. And no, I didn't have time to clean up. I hope you enjoy the odor of shrimp and ambition. It's been so very long since I've had a neural visitor. I hope you're back to eating seafood. In short, please only read this book while naked, blasting music so loud it throbs. I want you here so badly, but if this doesn't sound scintillating to you, if you have delicate sensibilities, or are not a fan of largescale emotion, the grotesque or the absurd, I suggest you get off here. *This is not for you.*

4. Interstellar Adventure

The poet H.D. wrote a series of three books examining war and unrest as a potential space of creativity and renewal during World War II, published as *Trilogy* in 1973. The sound of her typewriter was at times indistinguishable from gunfire. The first book opens with the poet walking around a recently bombed city, defending against the charge that, in the face of seismic events, poets are useless. She journeys through different times and spaces, fusing history and the present—the ruins of Egypt and a modern London—in search of what meaning can be assembled from the broken pieces of a city that has recently been through so much. *Trilogy* reminds readers of the role of the writer to record and help process complex realities, particularly when times get tough. In her *Helen in Egypt*, H.D. revises the mythology of the Trojan War from Helen's perspective—taking the epic form for women. Through all her work, she uses the monstrous as a way of talking about trauma, wonder, creativity, and transformation. All of which I want to think about here.

However, H.D.'s noble project doesn't change how absurdist the daily routine of any writer actually is. For Career Day my daughter wants to go as a writer, so should I send her in Virginia Woolf pajamas with a ballpoint pen, a mountain of debt, professional envy, grandiose aspirations, a hundred empty Chinese food containers, and a Submittable account to refresh all day, or take a less honest route?

She's off to a good start, though, listening endlessly to *Junie B. Jones* audiobooks. See, Junie is wise because she marvels at the surreal mechanics of this constructed life and breaks all grammar rules. Sometimes I want to tell my students to do the same, but I can't because, in addition to creative writing, I teach college composition, and it just wouldn't be a useful way to send them out into the world. And just what sort of world is it that I'm sending them out to? What if we could board a mythical bird and see the trajectory of our lives from above, understand our existence in this new, layered way? Would it help?

My daughter pops back into the room. She's wearing my bra on her head and using a banana that has seen better days as a microphone, as she belts out "Under Pressure" from the movie *Sing*. Her body wiggles to music she hears in her head. It's chilling to hear these adult concepts coming out in her squeaky little toon voice, most of which I can't make out at first: *It's the terror of knowing what this world is about / Watching some good friends screaming, 'Let me out!' / Pray tomorrow gets me higher / Pressure on people, people on streets.* She mis-says most of it, transforming it into another language entirely. I only fully find out what she's saying when I Google the lyrics and feel unnerved.

She does a complex, three-part curtsy-bow combination. When I clap for her, she instructs me to ask for an *encore*. Which I do. She does the curtsy-bow things again. I don't know how long this will go on. Time moves in entirely different ways when I'm with my kids. When I hang out with them, a microcosm inflates over us, and I wonder if the rest of the world can still see us. Hours can pass in minutes. Since they were born, I'm Rip Van Winkle, just waking up on a hill time and again, like *where the hell is everybody?*

5. *Ulysses* of Ladykind

Where am I writing to you from, exactly? Although I'd prefer an interstellar adventure, I'm currently right here, on an Earth grappling with so much. I'm not H.D. in London during the Blitz. I'm in my duplex apartment in Brooklyn, still in bed, now having transitioned to playing *My Little Pony* unicorn dress-up with my daughter under the covers, and who can eat more eggs (me!) with my son.

I've said we're not allowed to eat in the room, so he's just delivering whole boiled eggs into my mouth as a regulatory workaround. Whenever I finish one, I poke my unicorn horn out of the covers to dictate a little more of this into my phone until my daughter summons me back to the land of Equestria. In fact, I'm mistaken. She wants me to clarify to you that I'm an *alicorn*, not a *unicorn*. Because she has made me wings…out of the blouse I was going to wear to teach today.

I have some bad news. Not even the *My Little Pony* universe is safe from dystopia. According to a write-up I read after the last movie my daughter and I watched together, even the magical land of Equestria has lost its magic: *Friendship and harmony have been replaced by paranoia and mistrust. And Ponies now live separated by species. Sunny—a feisty and idealistic young Earth Pony—is convinced there's still hope for this divided world, but her slightly misguided and often hilarious efforts to change hearts and minds have led to her being branded a misfit. Sounds* familiar. I've often played Sunny the Earth Pony to my reality's answer to Equestria.

This is not Equestria, but I still need to write my way through my own city that's taken a similarly dark-speculative turn. As you read this, the plague is already upon you. Good night and good luck. Start running. Or, rather, keep reading. Be here with me for the hours we have left.

Trouble is I simply don't have words yet for what I'm trying to do here: explode notions like genre, category, book. But I don't just want to destroy stuff. My whole thing is to take all these already exploded pieces and build a new form from all I'm grappling with as I write: motherhood, writing, a global pandemic, and assorted other sociocultural calamities, this rapidly spinning ride called being alive right now. The answer comes to me while attempting to use expired cold medicine to save the world. To find my way into this goblin narrative, in addition to eating many eggs with my son, I read through a heritage of writers trying to do what I'm attempting: city walkers, monster makers, culture tellers, trauma warriors, class clowns, ghost story peddlers, finding new ways of surviving by playing fast and loose with textual time and space. And let's not forget my favorite: the obsessives.

Obsession is the only way I know how to relate to anything that moves me. I don't even need to be that into you to read through twenty pages of your Google search results. I'm a scholar and researcher even of the turds people leave in public toilets. I can't seem to avert my eyes. It's not how I was constructed. But I think this method, of keeping my eyes open long after others have shuttered theirs, has made me an explorer of the world's official undercarriage; the clue is often hidden in the caboose. What's crucial to my way of thinking is to decompose in order to recompose, always in the interest of creating new forms, even if they are made out of metaphorical turds, which is another reason I thought I might find goblin DNA when I sent away for the results.

I want to tell my goblin story about the minutiae but with epic aspirations. Is that even possible? But how to write a *Ulysses* of ladykind when I'm just one lady and no James Joyce? Please note that when I use terms such as *woman, lady, girl,* I mean no essentialist gender garbage but am speaking of whomever might like to go by those outdated monikers; in particular, I am referring to Wombats on Kangaroo Island. This story is for the weird girls, the weird boys, the weird not-quite-sures, for everyone who wants it. But I will say it might be hard to relate if you weren't the type who was picked on in middle school.

This is my epic journey. As Joey Soloway says, what if the heroine's journey moves less in an arc and more in spirals or circles? Is it a labyrinth? If so, how to explore it, and am I the architect or Minotaur? To answer these questions, I seek out mazes, memory palaces, and the architecture of our insides and outsides. I begin mapping my inner and outer city. I start to anatomize Goblin. My door is open a slant, and I can see my daughter peering in, just one eye, a Cyclops, child of the sea god Poseidon, one of the architects of Olympus.

6. No Cartoon Bluebirds

Last week had moved along in the normal manner (like lots of dishes to do and there were no cartoon bluebirds but that was okay), but I could feel the rumble of something coming. I taught my students with all the idealism that should have burned off by then and took copious care of my two children. To illustrate the professional-parental divide: parenting is an all-the-time-job that's taught me radical chaos, peace negotiation, patience with scooters, tenderness for anything that hurts, and how to make melon balls, but I still can't put it on my resume. Still, I like my two jobs since I enjoy bringing together the dense, absurdist, incomprehensible, hermetic spheres of parenting and writing/academia by losing sleep at night applying postcolonial theory to Paw Patrol.

I was torn between what, when I became a mother, had suddenly seemed like the striated worlds of my domestic sphere and my professional sphere—especially since so much of both took place in the same sphere of me at the kitchen table, with a messy bun and probably pink eye for the hundredth time that month from these little hooligans whom I adore and fear in equal measures. Plus, there are other conflicts. I made a recurring calendar reminder to submit something/anything writing-related every day at eight pm, but that's my time to stress-eat my kids' frozen Oreo stash with the door locked so nobody disturbs my cookie time, and I fear these two impulses may have an epic battle for power that destroys us all. Maybe that would happen this week.

My daughter pokes her head into the room, and I ask her what this book should be about, and she says about being her mom. My son hears us talking and bursts in with counsel. He advises me to write down the stuff I do every day but with ancient monsters and superheroes. Sounds like a real potboiler. He's currently reading *Percy Jackson* and some egghead (takes one to know one) relative gave him an illustrated children's version of *Ulysses*. Where did he even find that? On the dark web? And, to put it mildly, *Ulysses* is a lot to live up to.

"James Joyce Dies; Wrote 'Ulysses'" is how the *New York Times* summed up Joyce's life in his obituary headline because it was just that big of a deal. It certainly was to me. I read the book like I was trying to exhume his body, as though breaking the code of his powerfully, poetically difficult text—about history, politics, life, death, dirty jokes, loss, parents, children, creativity, and the very structure of time, space, thought and the city—could bring him back to life.

My son's back because he wants to play offline Minecraft. Offline Minecraft is when I won't let them do screens yet but they want to, so we create a low-tech version of this videogame where you can shape a three-dimensional world. The low-fi version of Minecraft involves us under the covers still, but now with Grimkeeper LEGOS that come with story-led building instructions. We never go by those stories but make up our own, and this time it's all about a mean gnome mom who won't let her kids play real Minecraft. I voice the mother like Yoda, with his grammatical proclivities and even do his speech: *My ally is the Force, and a powerful ally it is. Life creates it, makes it grow. Its energy surrounds us and binds us. Luminous beings are we, not this crude matter. You must feel the Force around you; here, between you, me, the tree, the rock, everywhere, yes.* They don't get the reference but laugh hysterically, until my daughter almost flips off the bed. *You must feel the Force around you*, I say again, just to make sure everybody heard.

After setting out to write the tale of wandering my post-pandemic city and having all the ideas (sounds like a page-turner, eh?) I start trying to find some epic structure I worshipped to riff on: *Ulysses* and then also *The Odyssey*? A feminist rewrite? A feminist drive-by? But then wasn't I just being insufferably pretentious? Also, filtering whatever I had to say through two sets of man doors and wasn't it time I find my own language? But how on earth to do that? Especially since if you don't please as a woman, some say you transform into dust motes visible only in certain sunny rooms. And Forbes.com says most dust motes are merely unsafe microplastics, so there you have it. Being a woman writer, it seems, is positively unsafe these days. But Goblin says I should do it anyway.

7. Freytag's Pyramid

I was imagining the conventional arc this story should have, the realizations and consequent transformations, the Freytag's Pyramid of it all, but then no. Maybe my book needs to be engineered inside-out, about how to unbuild that and rebuild something else, storytelling but in reverse, a memoir written by my fascicles, above all: different ways of seeing. The inside story of a woman.

I just want to tell my students so concerned about literary propriety: there are other narrative shapes and possibilities. Replace this wizened pyramid with a structure that better reflects the mess that is your life; so, say hello to the rollercoaster that is my chaotic living labyrinth built entirely out of Barbie Band-Aids, dusty books, old *I Love Lucy* episodes, Sponge Bob figurines and chicken fingers. When I advise writing students to read everything, they imagine only ancient tomes, but all those tweets, cereal boxes, news stories, and subtitled movies find their way into the layering structures of writing over time and reflect how we actually think and speak.

I want a mapmaker to one day chart that space where terrible writing suddenly turns into something that for a matter of minutes glows beyond words. Yesterday I walked half an hour out of my way to get coffee at a Park Slope Cafe called Muse because I truly believe this place has mystical inspirational properties. No, you're superstitious. In an early draft of his novel *Stephen Hero*, Joyce describes an epiphany as, *a sudden spiritual manifestation, whether in the vulgarity of speech or of gesture or in a memorable phase of the mind itself...the most delicate and evanescent of moments.* But, unlike Joyce, I'm no maker of epics. If anything, I suffer from the very modern disease of being a Medieval miniaturist in a world that values only literary maximalism. If it values literature at all.

And then how to title my book if I did write it? Being a very deep person, I took to social media and wrote a cheeky post *The title of the book I don't have time to write about how I spend half my life filling out CAPTCHAs: 'I'm Not a Robot Remember Me.'* But then I started thinking seriously about existence. Okay, so I wasn't a robot (that I'm aware of), but what was I? Human, as far as I knew. But what was the meaning of a human life? With the emergence of ChatGPT eliciting crucial questions about what makes a human or constitutes explicitly human writing, and the pandemic causing me to consider mortality in a less theoretical way, I decided, before I kicked the bucket, to write an actual version of this speculative book that existed first as a joke, for the sake of an attention-grabbing tweet, just one more lone howl in the virtual wilderness. And here we are, folks.

My daughter flips off the bed for real this time but is fine. I credit gymnastics class. She runs out and then back in, this time wearing a vampire cape and a Spiderman mask. She chides me, saying it's time to stop talking into my phone under the covers. She's probably right. I ask her what kind of superhero she is, and she says she's herself but from yesterday. I have no idea what this means. I wonder if she's interested in time travel or actually a character from the past. Ever the rationalist, my son asks her how she's standing here if she's from yesterday, and she says she has learned to be in two places at the same time. She has become a woman.

8. The Monster at the End of the Book

I don't fully freak out about my son's *we're all going to die someday* note because I'm accustomed to receiving such missives from him. There's no explanation for this. Though I've inquired with professionals. I attribute it, at least in part, to how we're living through a global pandemic, a civil rights meltdown, and one climate disaster after another such that it truly feels like end times. Just like Sesame Street's Grover, America was stunned to find that it itself was the monster at the end of the book. There's no explanation for this. Though I've inquired with professionals.

But the thing is that there's no god figure machined onstage to solve these manifold dilemmas for me because this isn't ancient Greek theater. There's just little old me, click-clacking away, my own voice echoing against an overstuffed city when I crack open my window to scream into the void. But in my early morning Prospect Park walk with the kids yesterday, I saw swans, in Brooklyn, and felt I was voyaging through the pages of great fiction. I'm going to interpret this as a surreal sign of better things to come. Don't take this away from me.

My son pokes his head in, says he doesn't need zombie pancakes but that I can play him in Plants Versus Zombies during screen time tonight. Lucky me. For those of you who don't know, screen time is the only time when parents take a break from being human jungle gyms. It takes a lot of willpower not to overdo it—on the part of the parents.

My daughter sprints in to scale me and then does a dramatic dismount, while announcing that she and my son are preparing a morning talent show. I have five minutes. It's only then that I notice she's wearing a homemade cat costume culled entirely from household items and recyclables from the bin. I try to contain it, but I break out laughing, and she looks mildly offended before becoming distracted by her toilet paper tail. She leaves the room, chasing her tail, while I continue to laugh, soundlessly, but so hard that I'll probably pop another blood vessel in my eye because I am so sexy.

I understand my son's darkly comedic mode of handling hard times because he gets it from me, an inheritance, or another plague, depending on how you look at it. It has been scientifically proven that when you laugh, a trap door opens in your brain that allows you to dwell in *uncertainties, mysteries, doubts, without any irritable reaching after fact and reason* that Keats crowed about hundreds of years ago. If you're not a Keats fan, which is fine by me, let me put it for you this way: if most writing is Google Maps, comedy is Waze, taking the side streets to the most vital part of the city and warning you about the cops along the way.

There's a special sense of humor that comes with growing up in New York and trying to navigate so many frustrating absurdities spiked with glints of the sublime. So comedy is part of my anatomization project because it helps me navigate the seriocomic vagaries of both city and brain. In her 2019 comedy special *Stage Fright*, Jenny Slate unforgettably depicts her brain as a crêpe made by a non-French cook, with a worm at its center who receives Slate's thoughts with panic. Slate tops it off by comparing the whole cerebral *mise en* scène to the bathhouse where spirits come to replenish themselves in Hayao Miyazaki's trippy animated film *Spirited Away.* In fact, with its meta-commentary on itself, and its transparent display of the comics' thinking, maybe comedy at its best *is* a brain, or a super-smart city that has gained consciousness.

After my kids go to bed, I watch stand-up, which I view as a peculiarly brilliant form of creative nonfiction and lyric essay, built as it is on coming at the problems of culture from a novel angle. There's something downright mesmerizing, for instance, about Cathy Park Hong's chronicling in *Minor Feelings* how binge-watching Richard Pryor's stand-up comedy enabled her to understand a whole set of emotions concerning race in America and her experience as the child of Korean immigrants. She labels these sentiments that Pryor unearths for her "minor feelings," or the toxic experience of being forced to question any negative racial emotions under the regime of the so-called American dream. By connecting her revelation concerning "minor feelings" to Pryor's work, Hong also elevates the often-undermined genre of stand-up comedy, offering it up as a mode with much truth-telling potential when it comes to sociopolitical matters. It's also pretty funny to picture Hong randomly doing impromptu stand-up comedy when people came expecting a poetry reading, as she tells it in the book. Since many poetry readings are boring (mine especially), this may not be such a bad idea to liven things up.

9. Comedy Tolerates the Miraculous

My kids often laugh after seeing something incredible but also after getting hurt. Humor is a top-notch way to cope with tragedy but also with wonder, which is why Wylie Sypher said, *comedy tolerates the miraculous.* Yes, we must cope with the wondrous because it asks that our tiny brains suddenly grow in stunning ways to intake it. It's like how in the Greco-Roman tales, mortals couldn't look directly at gods lest their heads explode. But my whole literary project involves chasing things that could possibly make my head explode—while staying safe for my kids, who still need me to reach things on high shelves.

How have I survived the pandemic? In part, through my pitch-black, slapstick-surrealist tendency to find humor anywhere, laughing instead of crying at least some of the time, seeing the situation from any available uncanny angle. At the same time, it's crucial to stay grounded, which is a piece of cake for me since I'm always embarrassing myself. Maybe I also cherish comics because I have always inadvertently been one myself.

Case in point: In a recent composition class, I taught an essay on the strangeness of embalming, discussed funeral practices, and ended up somehow making a joke in which I invited students to attend my future funeral. In case you were feeling self-conscious about public speaking, I'm here to tell you that I also realized after that same class that I'd lost an earring, which means I'd invited Freshmen to my funeral while wearing one hoop in my ear…like a pirate.

My kids get sick of waiting and come into my room to do the talent show for me while I'm still lying supine in bed, now wrapped tightly in my covers by my daughter. She says, *let's pretend she's a mummy.* I can barely breathe. After the lackluster talent show that involves some gyrating and general farm animal antics, I clap so hard my hands hurt because I can see they are expecting it. My son asks for a standing ovation, but I tell him I'm wrapped too tightly for that right now. I'm apparently also the talent show judge. I declare a tie, and break dramatically out of my mummy wrappings. I then provide them with medals made from bottle caps that I quickly color with markers to make them more festive. My children act like I've given them the queen's jewels.

The current absurd behavior I'm working on putting a stop to is awkwardly hugging people I don't know very well, who don't seem like they really want to be hugged. The need to do so bubbles up in me and then I lie awake at night wondering why I hugged the shy writer who almost cowered. Now, when I approach people, I do so with my arms firmly at my sides lest I should be hit with a wave of inexplicable warmth that will embarrass me later.

My description of the hugging issue is also related to another uncomfortable thing, which is also maybe just called being a writer: my sincere problem with TMI, and how I must remind myself to just stop when I start flippering my mouth, spurting details nobody needs to know, least of all the guy at the falafel stand, kind and patient though he may be. And really because he's kind and patient, I shouldn't punish him by frothing at the mouth about my UTI. I find myself wishing I could go back and retroactively edit most things I say in public, and here on the page. Which is all to say I cherish comics because the whole point is to say too much and make people uncomfortable…but in a good, intellectually transformative, way.

10. Neapolitan Pasta Varietals in the Anthropocene

The door to my room swings open but nobody is standing there. I'm scared for a minute but then a fleet of paper airplanes drifts in, followed by a single water balloon that explodes on the already cracked wood floor. I yell at the kids, but they can't hear me over the roar of two *Captain Underpants* audiobooks playing in the other room simultaneously. More paper airplanes. When I go to pick one up and unfold it, just knowing there will be a missive, it says, *get out of bed mommy!* It's still not yet six in the morning.

To try to understand more about the comedic connections forming in my head, I read—on my iPhone Libby app as more paper airplanes drift in and the ceiling leaks on my head—Sianne Ngai on how the *zany* is often the experience of the woman *confronted by—and endangered by—too many things coming at her at once.* Sounds about right. Now a water balloon lands inches away. *That's it*, I scream, but still don't leave my room or move out of the way of the leak. I just reach under the mattress, unearth an old candy bar, and eat it in a single gulp.

How do I handle being irritated, overwhelmed, or invaded? For one thing, I switch on my tendency to imagine ridiculous things happening around people who are being unpleasant to me. Last week, I visualized (the passions of my son and daughter coalescing in this spectacle) an alicorn playing Chess over the head of the guy mansplaining the works of Elena Ferrante to me.

I also daydreamed delivering the most asinine response possible, just to confirm his estimation of my intellectual faculties, along the lines of, *for me, Ferrante's oeuvre really hinges on the notion of Neapolitan pasta varietals in the Anthropocene.* Take it from me: it's always good, in academic debates, to throw in any mention of the *Anthropocene* for good measure. You're welcome.

Humor and writing have always been my ways out. Like how, ever since childhood, I've imagined funny things, or even agents of salvation, over the heads of anyone who was hurting me. I would write little scripts in my head for how the moment could go differently. This may be when I first started seeing my lady Goblin. The beginning of how I came to survive by rewriting reality, playing with time, space, and narrative in the name of metamorphosis. In the name of: *just don't do that to a kid, okay? Okay?!* When kids are hurt, it messes with their machinery in perpetuity. So, they must spend the rest of their lives rebuilding these mechanisms. But they will never be quite the same. Does this mean that these mechanisms are smaller afterward? Not necessarily. What if they grow larger after the astonishing process of survival? Where is *that* trauma narrative? I have yet to read it.

My son comes in, apologizes for the water balloon and paper airplane offensive and asks if I want to play walnut chess. Walnut chess is where you replace all the chess pieces with walnuts that you distinguish from one another with a Sharpie. He wins every time because he's good at chess and at deciphering which walnut chess piece is which. I tell him that some say chess is a stand-in for war, originally used to educate Persian princes about battle tactics, but he just checkmates me and then literally eats my walnut King.

11. My Beloved Goblin

As a kid, when something bad was happening to me, I went into battle mode, imagining what I thought of as my beloved Goblin. I wasn't sure if what I saw was what a goblin was supposed to look like and, in theory, I knew goblins weren't real. But, nevertheless, every time I needed her, there she was: with glossy black fur, slimy, fierce, maternal, hovering over whatever it was to help me through it. I knew rationally she probably wasn't there, but this didn't stop her from saving my life. And wasn't she just an early form of writing?

Yet, no matter what happened to me, I retained a protected inner space. I would picture being surrounded by this purple light that emanated from Goblin, within which nobody could truly touch me. I realize this was just a coping mechanism, but what a blessing to feel you can carry something inside that nobody can touch, an interior bioluminescence. I still hold it in my body through subway commutes where I'm not sure if someone's going to get violent, an illumination that mentally teleports me, these days, back home to my kids. Then, while whatever badness goes on around me, there I am with my children, playing Monopoly. I'm always the hat. You could be beating me to a pulp, but I'd be buying up Boardwalk. I find out years later from a therapist that this is called visualization and it helps with post-traumatic stress disorder.

My daughter returns to the room, knocks over the walnut chess board, setting off my son, who storms out of the room. Before I can follow him, she tells me she has made me something to apologize for the water balloons. She orders me to close my eyes and then deposits something sticky in my hand. When I look down, I find two pink Starbursts taped together, with toothpicks inserted as limbs. The starbursts appear to be holding hands, and their hands are made of tiny pieces of their own Starburst bodies. She says, *it's me and you all the time mommy.* I think it's sweet until I let myself wonder where she got Starbursts in the morning. My son stomps in, now angry that she has raided his backpack Starburst stash. I ask him where he got them, but he tells me he's taking this one to the grave. Where did he learn that saying? Now I'm cleaning up the walnuts with sticky Starburst hands. But as I do it, I notice the other two Starburst she has shaped as hearts and left on my pillow. She tells me to eat them and I do.

I have retained this habit of finding, during whatever atrocity, the one shining something that gets me through. In this way, my "cheerfulness" is not shallow or phony but the most real thing I have, and very much a weapon of survival, my way of importing something of the underworld, feeding blood to ghosts so they can give me wisdom, as Odysseus did.

It's also a fairy wand that I wield in the face of those who attack me, shouting *hocus pocus* until that motherfucker runs off. Because here's something else I have discovered: you can beat someone up with a fairy wand if necessary.

12. This is For You

There are people who respond to being hurt by hurting everyone, and those who will spend the rest of their lives obsessively trying to make sure nobody is hurt ever. Both are impossibilities. It's not possible to hurt everyone, nor is it possible to save everyone. Nor is it my job to save everyone. But tell my psyche that.

At night I roam the cityscape, collecting everyone being harmed and putting them in my kangaroo pouch, my dusty old womb that my kids aren't even using anymore, the one my OB-GYN told me was *unicornuate*, or with only one working fallopian tube, well of course it is. One day I will tell my daughter that I have a unicorn womb and she will do a dance of joy. So, whoever you are, if you are suffering, if anyone is hurting you, please feel free to take refuge in my deformed unicorn womb. *This is for you.*

My daughter drags the Twister board into my room. She has placed a clementine over every dot, and googly eyes on every clementine. I ask her what this contraption is. She says, *I'm watching you*, and leaves.

I frequently imagine engaging in time travel, going back as I am now to confront my past doer of harm. I'm often wearing some sort of superhero get-up. There's usually an intergalactic battle. There are a lot of set pieces that we destroy. I say to him, *hi again, I've put myself back together with the wisdom of broken things, having seen where the goblin slinks off to die, like the exact geolocation, but, surprise! I did not die there. I said, no thank you, and dragged myself back, now part-goblin, and all-writer, ready to write the beyond.*

What's more, I have the kind of daughter who made my Bonsai tree a bird so it would have a friend, and the kind of son who covers me with a blanket and makes me tea when I look like I'm about to combust. It guts me to think of anyone ever hurting them. I want to be this wearable stuffed animal that goes places with them just to make sure they're okay at any given time. Their Goblin. But I must let them leave the house without wearing me as a teddy bear. This is called finding a healthy balance. It's just one more impossible thing about parenting and being alive that I attempt daily. But since I've visited the land of the dead, tasted its briny fruits, I now know that, flawed as it is, human existence does indeed have many forms of wonder worth holding onto. Like how my son told me Minecraft has a new update with cherry blossoms, or how there's a harpist who plays in my father's hospital while he's getting chemo and radiation.

13. Who Gives a Fuck About an Oxford Comma?

My knowledge of the origins of my son's macabre comedy sense (me!) doesn't stop me from spending the rest of the post-letter day worrying while attempting to decode my complex child. Plus, I understand his philosophical sentiment. What a cruel joke that we have all been placed on this earth and told it was inevitable. One day we *will* all die. But we can never know when, and there's nothing we can do about it. It's torture. But, as I often tell my students, this is also what gives life its poignancy, its mini doses of astonishment. I get this from my mom who has a certain, as I learned to say in high school French class, *joie de vivre*. Plus, as Bill Murray, the ultimate philosopher, demonstrated in *Groundhog Day*, eternal life just might be the worst.

My phone has locked and gone dark. I touch it back to life and open Outlook, Gmail, Instagram, Facebook (because I am old now), and Twitter, to find limitless emails, and updates from the virtual life I'm trying to run parallel to my own in which I'm just generally sparklier. An email I'd sent myself at 3:17 a.m. when I couldn't sleep: *start your book lazypants* and one that simply read, *sandwich*. No idea what that was about.

There are also many dispatches from concerned progressive organizations about our failed democracy, our nation that may or may not be sinking into the Nether, which in case you're not the parent of a 9-year-old, the Minecraft Wiki defines as *a dangerous hell-like dimension containing fire, lava, fungal vegetation, many hostile mobs, and exclusive structures and biomes.*

The kids are sad about their friend Anna moving away after her mom's restaurant closed during COVID. They want to do a puppet show featuring Anna as a character. They haul reams of paper, child-safe scissors, Scotch tape, and broken crayons into my room and dump it all onto my bed, as I'm trying to respond to the 4:13 a.m. email from one of my students. The whole text of the email is: *is everything going to be okay?*

The truth is that I don't know if everything is going to be okay for my kids, for my students, for my dad, for Anna. But I can't tell any of them that. So I fashion a puppet that resembles Anna perfectly and do the Yoda voice again, which gets no laughs this time. I'll admit I feel a little bereft about this. I'm nothing if not a panderer.

14. Zombie Apocalypse

Has taking the subway gotten more dangerous or am I just noticing it more now? I've been almost jumped twice in the last year. My local station at night is a ghost town, the perfect target for the zombie apocalypse. I receive an email from an academic press rep who wants to know if I'll be adopting their mad scientist composition textbook in future courses. Um, definitely. I don't write back about how I'm not sure about the status of future courses since, due to the whole zombie apocalypse situation going on in my world at large, I'm not a hundred percent certain there will be a future.

And really, as the recent *New Yorker* piece on the end of the English major indicates, we college English teaching folk weren't feeling super confident before all this because, as Vampire Weekend puts it, *who gives a fuck about an Oxford comma?* And what's our argument for why we deserve to survive? That we help young people do critical thinking, that reading builds empathy, that they can all be lawyers later? We have lost track.

Except I know it matters because in my Literature Across Cultures class this semester, they stay long after class ends to argue about Jamaica Kincaid's piece "Girl" and to grapple with ideas. In this class, they all come from different backgrounds, but they reach across to form something conceptually larger. Isn't that how education should work?

How our country should work? These students are so classy. They always manage to keep it civil, unlike the rest of America, which has already entered a second Civil War without most people even realizing it. People keep worrying that, at the rate we're going, the next Civil War will commence, and it's like, *buddy, it's already here.*

Several students who aren't enrolled in the class have started sitting in. We asked facilities to bring in extra chairs for them. Because it's so rare these days to have a civil conversation with people who disagree with you without violence erupting.

A fight has broken out in Puppetland. My daughter has commandeered the Anna puppet, who has now gone off the rails, and is trying to eat the Captain Underpants and Dog Man puppets. I say, *hey, what happened to Democracy?* But my kids just looked mystified, then go back to pummeling each other's avatars. Just like what's happening outside Puppetland. I comfort myself with this other message from Puppetland, or rather from Mr. Rogers: *When I was a boy and I would see scary things in the news, my mother would say to me, 'Look for the helpers. You will always find people who are helping.'* This has been my motto recently.

15. The Peanut Butter Game

I feel a little better because I can hear my kids playing the peanut butter game with our neighbor's sweet old dog, who has darted over for an early morning visit from across the hall. (We have an open-door policy with these neighbors because they are lovely, and we switch off cooking meals for each other.) I taught this game to my kids after watching the movie *Funny People*, which I think is underrated. What you do is put peanut butter on your face and let the dog lick it off. This game is genius. And can go on for hours.

As the dog licks their faces and they howl with delight, I pull my patched red chair up to the broken desk and attempt to write something more structured, but the world's exploding, which makes these ordered black symbols on white paper feel tenuous at best. What am I even trying to locate in this ritual anyway? An ancient idea of a muse speaking to me through centuries, providing the mystical written antidote to a world on fire? But what I really wish is that I could not write but just bottle the real things going on around me. What could be more real, more wonderful, than a dog licking peanut butter off a child's face? I want to give you this in the sort of bottle that washes up from sea with a message in it. But the message would not be written. It would just be the kid, the dog, the peanut butter. How do I do that? Please let me know.

I also don't tell the academic rep that she may find me on a mountaintop in a fortnight, having been torn to bits by all the eagles who attached themselves to my body parts and then flew in different directions. Instead, I inexplicably reply to her right now, at this still early hour, with an email so polite it makes my Southern mother proud somewhere. The world is intersectionally unspooling but somehow my first move is to make sure the academic press rep doesn't feel ignored.

The emails keep dinging in: various e-newsletters crowing about how AI will wipe out both my jobs—writing and teaching writing—in one fell swoop. I think the solution is clear: we must start writing papers for the chatbots that sound so human they get *them* in trouble with their teachers. The whole potential roboticization of my jobs is too much to take in right now, so I leave it aside, and roll over into the fetal position to wait until the bots find out nobody will read their books either.

But my daughter discovers me and pulls me into the living room to play the Peanut Butter Game. The dog named Trinity bounds over to see me, causing me to forget however briefly my measly Homo sapiens' problems. Our neighbor chose the name Trinity for the dog because he's a big *Matrix* fan, and I wonder if this dog can help us humans hack our way out of this ornate computer program. Before I can find out, Trinity nudges the open peanut butter jar until I dutifully spread some on my cheek and lie on my back. As her outlandish purple tongue unfurls above me with its Niagara Falls of drool, I prepare to be remade. I look up to find my daughter standing over us, taking a video of the whole thing on my iPad, looking at the dog and me like she has just witnessed a miracle. I reach for more peanut butter. As soon as my daughter is distracted, though, I scamper back into my room, with her and the dog in hot pursuit. I chuck a tennis ball out of my room to throw them both off my trail, and it works.

16. In Bed in Old Man Pajamas

My inbox floods with panicked emails from my students, and I feel personally responsible for each one of them. I sit in my old man pajamas and quickly answer the emails I can as a function of muscle memory—here's the student *New York Times* log-in, here's how to outwit the buggy campus WIFI, here's how to wake up in time for class. But how to answer the question that floats unsaid behind every email each student sends me (which is why I answer every single one of them, even if I must wake up early to do so, and even if it cuts into my own writing time): *How can I be a person in this world right now?*

I let my phone fall onto the bed as I puzzle over how to talk to my students about the state of the world when I'm no expert, and have perhaps never been able to interpret its peculiar signals, now more than ever, as we enter a phase that feels suddenly speculative. I'm all about departures from reality in the books I devour, eating domestic fabulism for breakfast. But I don't know how to read this shoddy science fiction called being alive right now. And where am I without my reading skills. Without my writing skills, what with AI already twice the writer I am. Without my teaching skills, as my jobs seem shaky at best? It's not like I have a single other useful skill, unless you count being able to spot a crisis but only once it's too late. In bed in old man pajamas. That's where.

I write back to all students I can't think of a response for yet, *let's talk more about this after class*, as a way of momentarily putting them off, yes—since I have failed to draw appropriate boundaries ever in my life and then must hastily erect them last minute, which is now. But I also mean it. I legitimately look forward to having these conversations with each of them. Though I nod with exhaustion at every negative tweet about academia's current shitshow, I find these talks with students to be the very thing that gets me to finally creak out of bed and get dressed this morning.

17. Introducing the Unicorn Princess

The shrill little cry I emit—as I try to re-pierce with an earring the hole in my ear that has mysteriously closed—summons my daughter yet again. I'm still upset about how sad all my students are. She shoves me on the bed and trapezes herself onto my back until I calm down. She flips me over and mushes her face against mine until I can feel the precipitation of her breathing. Let me tell you there is categorically no other feeling like this. I've looked everywhere. It's inimitable. In this close-up shot, her eyes are just blue horizons and I often hallucinate walking off into them. Something nobody tells you about parenting: sometimes *they* comfort *you*. Also, you may have the urge to walk off into the borderlands of their irises sometimes. No big deal.

She makes walrus sounds in my ear while nuzzling me, and I respond with my own squeaks and whimpers because this is how we find home. It's our secret language, and we would do it endlessly if it weren't for the real world with all its death and cutbacks and non-walrus material.

In all honesty, neither of us is sure what a walrus sounds like. But this is our interpretation of what we imagine it might sound like, or what we remember from a few animal shows. I believe this is what Jean Baudrillard was talking about with his *simulacra*, or copies without originals, but I might have gone high to the college philosophy class where we covered that one.

My son rushes in to see what's going on. He calls us walruses and nuzzles us. I know he's waiting for it, so I say, *introducing the Unicorn Princess,* because I forgot to say it when she woke up, as I do every single morning, because these little rituals hold us all together. At the point she awakes every morning, he's inevitably been up since before five, doing chess puzzles and assembling a sampling of the most bizarre foods in our kitchen for my breakfast.

When I pull her up off the bed and escort them both into the kitchen, I spot the centerpiece of my son's breakfast platter this morning, in addition to the eggs from earlier: the tiny pickles my mom brings him called *cornichons.* I stuff a few into my mouth as I email all my students back to let them know I haven't poofed away overnight along with their certainty about the future.

18. The Transfer Portal

Above all, I check that my student athlete who needs to switch schools is familiar with the NCAA transfer portal. Can it take him to another dimension, though? Unfortunately not. As I field more student emails about debt, depression, illness, pregnancy, and general loss of hope, I write back to remind them—as I try to do daily, when sending them jokes and poems at the bottom of their homework reminders—that, regardless of the turmoil, I'm here. *Introducing the Unicorn Princess.*

Here's the section of the Audre Lorde poem "Power" that I send students this morning: *Unless I learn to use / the difference between poetry and rhetoric / my power too will run corrupt.* Here's the section I don't send them: *The difference between poetry and rhetoric / is being ready to kill / yourself / instead of your children.*

I schedule pop-up office hours to help the students sort things out. I dial the one friend I know will be up to me unloading on her, but get distracted by a blanket moving seemingly by itself around the apartment. I wonder if it's our downstairs poltergeist, Gumby, which we (mostly) joke about, before I see it's just my daughter in her walrus blanket, and that I've left a voicemail of heavy breathing. But mostly what worries me is, *what kind of a lowlife leaves messages anymore?*

Gumby appeared as a character in our lives when our apartment started to creak more than usual. Our duplex is on the bottom floor of the apartment building and we can hear our neighbors creaking down the stairs, but this seemed different. There was an almost knocking sound in the walls, things went missing or appeared in other locations, furniture seemed to subtly shift positions. I ended up chalking it all up to an old apartment and having mischievous kids, but how to explain that they seemed scared too? I wondered if our house would soon become like the one in Mark Danielewski's *House of Leaves*, spawning monstrous labyrinthine tunnels. I would be pretty okay with that. But you know who else, in mythology anyway, have been known to perform acts of mischief such as knocking on walls and moving things in the house? Goblins.

An email from *Daily Dharma*, which I subscribed to on some night I hoped to become a more spiritual person. I don't unsubscribe, though, because I'm too spiritual. Instead, I carefully read the emails each day, even though they largely irritate me, in the hopes that this will bring me goodwill from the universe. The one for today is about opening myself to the sacred in the face of hardship, but I can't even with that right now. The closest I will get to the sacred today comes five minutes later when my daughter needs me to sit next to her and tell her a story while she uses the toilet.

19. Yet Another Bathroom Story

While telling my daughter yet another bathroom story about Goblin (there's a whole series I've created over the years), I text one work friend about whether she's ready to form a band of traveling writer minstrels and another about how the email we just received from facilities feels a little too on-the-nose: *Building Management is conducting tests of the fire alarm system today. Please disregard all that you may hear, see, or smell.* She's very funny and writes back, *I'm deceased.* I giggle but also envision for a moment that maybe she's being literal and trying to tell me that she's an actual ghost before pulling myself together as my daughter is successful at her task.

In the climate of college financial distress post-COVID, I'm freaking out about losing my first tenure-track job. Even though part of me knows this teaching job never belonged to me. Not for real. I look around at my apartment and children. None of this did. Nothing does. Not according to *Daily Dharma* and centuries of Buddhist thought.

I'm not sure where I stand on the matter of what it all means, what lurks beyond perception. Except to say that I believe in some nebulous something out there, despite all the obvious ugliness and evidence otherwise. I often feel it when someone is nice to me for no reason, or when I touch my daughter's thicket of curls, where I discover things that have been lost for centuries. During combative faculty assemblies,

I daydream about getting lost in her hair, of the supernatural items I might discover there, of how I might be able in this way to see what my daughter sees, feel what she feels, think what she thinks, or at least what her curls think. I'm sure her curls would be provocative thinkers.

20. Giant Blobs of Seaweed

Now out of the bathroom, while we all eat the tiny pickles together, my son asks, *did you find the note funny?* I struggle with how to answer. I go with: *I found it funny the way it's funny when cartoons hit other cartoons with mallets.* He nods like what I said is wise. We recommence eating the pickles.

Meanwhile, in comes the third email this week from someone's daughter's friend's dental hygienist's father-in-law asking whether I can read his three-thousand-page novel by tomorrow and ensure immediate publication along with a place on the *New York Times* Bestseller List. I wonder if he knows I must set an alarm each day to find time to shower or that my last book was published by a small press and largely used as a bar napkin. Now, there's that alarm reminding me to take my shower. But I still forget because the kids are now trying to cook their own zombie pancakes. I rush to turn off the stove, put out a small paper towel fire, and lecture them on kitchen safety and a little something called adult supervision. It's a wonder we all survive in this apartment together.

Here comes an alert from NPR about a nonagenarian turtle named Mr. Pickles who has just become a parent. How lovely for him. Then another NPR alert: *Giant blobs of seaweed are hitting Florida. That's when the real problem begins.* Wonderful. I don't so much live as collect all the bizarreness around me and excrete it in written form. Please put that on my gravestone. (I'm surprised I haven't already made a joke asking my freshmen writing class to do so.) It often ends up as a pile of neon slime on pages nobody ever sees. But they tell me this is called a writing career, so I cash my small checks and keep teaching in an MFA program.

I jump vigorously on the tiny trampoline with my girl while singing John Denver's "Take Me Home, Country Roads" for my boy, who spends a lot of time listening to old music with his grandparents. I attempt to feed, wash, and clothe the kids while grading all the papers and doing all the lesson planning that I didn't get to the night before, which is pretty much all of it. And the upshot is that nobody gets washed yet.

I want to find time this morning to write a heavy tome that helps America process the maze of its history that led to these batty sociopolitical, ecological, psychological, scatological, eschatological times, but I keep getting distracted by my daughter running around with my granny underwear on her head. I ask what happened to my bra and she says she outgrew it. She's growing up so fast.

Now, as I title this word document, *Heavy Tome*, the kids start in for the day on the bathroom humor, and it really isn't all that far off in the end. To consider the riddle of existence from a more jovial perspective: do you really think it's a mistake that eschatological, or *any system of doctrines concerning last, or final, matters, as death, the Judgment, the future state*, is so close to scatological, or *the study of or preoccupation with excrement or obscenity*? That is to say, the ultimate ending of humankind is very closely concerned with curses and feces. I'm comforted to know that it will all end in poop. This makes sense to the mother in me.

As I prepare to write the first word of my *Heavy Tome*, I get an email from my dream press saying they won't be publishing my book that's currently out on submission right now, but thanks for entrusting them with it. I no longer trust them further than I can throw them. What the parenting books don't cover: how to find it in yourself to get a big writing rejection and then still sing all the songs from *Frozen* in a Peppa Pig voice while trying to put on makeup that doesn't look like your daughter did it. Which she did.

I notice a text my friend has sent at two in the morning. She wants to know if I have a morning-after pill. Why would I just have that lying around? She has added emojis of a baby and a skull. I don't respond now because I know she's still sleeping.

21. Where the Wild Things Are

By seven antemeridian, the kids and I have already done finger painting, enacted whole parts of *Where the Wild Things Are*, cleaned up still more broken things, and invented a secret language. I don't tell them this but, spoiler alert, they've simply invented…Pig Latin.

My daughter is intrepid. In the case that my son and I are accidentally too rough with her during a pillow fight or wrestling match, both of which we've also already done this morning, she'll pop back up like a videogame creature, and say, *Meep,* or some other cartoonish thing. This morning I have also consulted the orbiting mental repository where I keep all the information about our family's physical, philosophical, and emotional needs for the day, year, and entire future, and checked Facebook, Twitter, BookTok, and Instagram 6 times, but only because I'm busy.

I've read to them and told them countless tales already this morning. I make for them a land just on the horizon. A collector of mental spaces, I know only too well what this world will be for them—a cerebral holiday, a brain vacation, a space they can rise to in their minds, safe and warm when the world hassles them or beats them to a pulp, as the world has been known to do, as it has done for centuries, as it will continue to do—so I help to create for them a burrow for when things get even harder, a Goblin.

While the kids busy themselves again with the tiny pickles and just generally breaking my house, I try to take that quick shower I forgot about earlier, while listening to a *Modern Love* podcast for the podcasting class I'm teaching, on a Guantanamo prisoner making friends with an iguana that he considers to be elegant, and I remember how virtuosic humans are, how they can reinvent themselves to fit any given tragedy, find the holy in the hellish, and make connections wherever possible. An iguana seems an excellent place to start.

My daughter yanks back the shower curtain to scream that she's lonely and tell me I look scary when I'm wet. I don't have time to wash my hair, and I just skim the most relevant parts of the text, so to speak, as my son yells that he's going to do WWF wrestling with his sister now, and I hurry to get out of the shower.

In my rush, I drop the soap, slip while trying to retrieve it, and cut my cheek in two places on the spigot, so that I will now be teaching all my classes this morning with an x-scar on my face like Jack Sparrow. I have now completed my transformation into a pirate. The kids will be thrilled.

22. Twirling into Science Fiction

In the year 2020, after receiving an "Adjunct for Life" T-shirt for the holidays (I found it hilarious, mostly), peak-pandemic, with no childcare, I got the tenure-track job I'd been pursuing all those years. I grew up reading novels about writers and professors—even the Nabokovian ones that portrayed this lifestyle as patently cruel and absurd—and I still wanted in.

I'd left my apartment in Brooklyn by six-thirty every morning for years to teach my eight-thirty classes in the Bronx; then rode two trains in the afternoon to teach more writing in Sugar Hill, where I'd also lived in grad school. I marveled at the literary history of this neighborhood—which Langston Hughes called *that attractive rise of bluff,* where Ralph Ellison wrote *Invisible Man*—as I walked Convent Avenue, past all the churches and the shop with the good coffee and a different cleverly chalked sign each day. You must find that shop with the good coffee in each new neighborhood. You don't really know the area until you do. I feared my squiggly lines would overflow the container of the proper academic if I ever did attain my dream, but this didn't change the fact that I was wildly jubilant when I finally got the job we were told, on the first day of our PhD program, we would never get.

But then came that unreal time. COVID, Omicron, among others, and the raw deal of a variant named after one of the Greek letters my mom helped me memorize as a kid. The sensation of *Omicron* on my tongue totally different this time around because the association had changed, like our city, altered to the point of becoming alternate.

In the early days of COVID I inhaled online articles with such snappy, apocalyptic headlines as *Top 20 Horrific Pandemic Movies to Watch While You're Quarantined*. We were frightened, faced with the unknown, suddenly living in a state of *lockdown*, performers in the movie *Contagion* without our knowledge, our life suddenly cinematic, our flesh rapidly becoming celluloid. But, when my brain was disassembled yet again by my daily life twirling off into science fiction, I think it came back more prepared to wrap itself around the unthinkable.

23. The Angel of History

How it was slow, then sudden, then forever. How now it's our life. Is this always how it will be? Our children growing up thinking of intimacy, of other kids, as danger? More than any other event in our lives (besides September eleventh, of course, when one of the planes flew past my mother's office window, and she just watched, dumbfounded as disaster struck), it has shown us how easily catastrophe happens, the ease with which normal situations can just slink into calamity. After a tragedy of this scale, all our lives become myth.

We are always living in/through history, but it becomes more palpable during these sorts of upheavals, its outlines suddenly visible. Sometimes I picture what Junie B Jones might say about all this—COVID, my father being sick, the meaning of life—since my daughter listens to her audiobooks, while she makes an art mess, until they become my own mental soundtrack. I always wonder what Goblin would say.

The shock of the plague vibrating through our various communities real and imagined. Every social media thread and conversation looping back to meditations on the apocalypse as we tried to locate some significance in the wreckage. I started learning different ways of using words like *zoom* and *pod*, groping to navigate this new linguistic ecosphere. But I stammered over the word *pandemic* every time because it felt too clinical to address the chaos and crackle of lived bodily experience here in Brooklyn.

Instead, to talk about this time, I will summon a ghost, or maybe another goblin, as this writer is dead and a specialist of the haunted nature of histories. I will call upon Walter Benjamin's description of the angel of history to help us think about now, and I humbly request that you hold this image in your mind while reading the rest of this book: *His face is turned toward the past. Where we perceive a chain of events, he sees one single catastrophe which keeps piling wreckage upon wreckage and hurls it in front of his feet. The angel would like to stay, awaken the dead, and make whole what has been smashed. But a storm is blowing from Paradise; it has got caught in his wings with such violence that the angel can no longer close them. The storm irresistibly propels him into the future to which his back is turned, while the pile of debris before him grows skyward. This storm is what we call progress.* Because I spend so much time with kids, when I read this, I picture Sunny, the My Little Pony who still has hope for a now-dystopian Equestria.

When we did finally get COVID, my daughter was first. We had my son sleep upstairs while I wore a mask and clung to my crying daughter all night, shooing my son away every time he came to try to hug his sister, who called out for him the entire night. He calls her his girl and, frankly, helps me parent all the time. When we finally ascended the stairs that next morning, he was camping out at the top, holding a picture of the virus, imagined as a cartoon villain that he was eviscerating with a sword. While I don't condone dismemberment, dare I say it was pretty touching as far as slaughter goes.

After we recovered, she talked about what she called the *wirus* incessantly, taking a cue from her brother, and understanding it largely in the vernacular of animated baddies. She peeked around every corner in case the *wirus* was about to jump out, a Dr. Evil looking to hijack some nuclear weapons and hold the world hostage for one million dollars. But, she kept telling me, she wasn't scared of the *wirus* because her brother would save her every time. I asked how. *With his chess board.* It turned out he'd told her she could use it as a shield next time.

24. Effusing into the Void

In September 2020, I was teaching in a hybrid format—on Zoom but also in person—so that my vulnerable population of first-year and first-generation students didn't decamp during this global disaster. I filled out a health form and had my temperature taken by a robot machine each morning. I tried to show students I was smiling, crinkle-eyed, behind my mask and face shield. I performed emotive acrobatics to prevent us all from sliding into a breathless darkness, and to bond with students from behind layers of plastic and electrostatic non-woven polypropylene fiber. I learned to read their moods by eye motion and skin crease alone and the rare stab of laughter. I gave them everything I had because how else do you live? My son always reminds me to *soak it all in*.

One of my colleagues described Zoom teaching as *effusing into the void*. My kids were also going to school on Zoom, and I'd joined a *pod* with other parents where we took turns facilitating these *online learning sessions*, which mostly meant I sweated all over children after I chased them down and plopped them back in front of their Zoom screens when they escaped and just generally became a professional fruit juice mixologist. Sometimes I had to facilitate one of my kids' Zoom school sessions while also running one of my own, which involved all of us at the same kitchen table yelling into screens and nobody feeling heard.

A dystopian strain of disconnection ran through those semesters no matter how many workshops on student engagement we were required to attend. Since students had to wear masks in class, and we weren't allowed to require them to turn on their Zoom cameras, I never saw most of their full faces.

I have never grown more tired of my own face: its vampiric too-pale skin and dark hair, my own beakiness peering back at me daily. It was just me and my own pedagogy. The space of the class altered in hair-raising ways that transformed into a cruel joke Geoffrey Sirc's otherwise visionary call to make the classroom a place that gives *its inhabitants a sense of the sublime.* You should see my students' faces, though, when I introduce them to Sianne Ngai's concept of "stuplimity," that strange mixture of boredom and astonishment, and they suddenly have a word for the last few years.

After they dropped the subway mask mandate, for a week I marveled at each facial detail and found every single person on the train wildly attractive. That almost too poignant instant when someone you've never seen without a mask bares their face, that contraband skinscape with its long-lost expanse of nose-mouth-chin, and you don't know whether to laugh or cry. Even though I'd never seen most of their faces in their entirety, I always recognize my students from that time now when I see them maskless on campus. Because when you stare at someone's eyes while living through a time of death together, you remember.

When my kids finally stopped wearing masks at school, my daughter told me her teacher looked different when her face was naked. *What did you imagine beneath?* I'd asked. *Another mask.*

25. When Will the Unicorn Die?

In those first two years of COVID, death was everywhere. I made my way to teach each morning through a boarded-up downtown Brooklyn readying itself for riots, passed daily a public art exhibit featuring the names of the deceased tumbling over one another. There were mass graves on, of all names, Hart Island.

On my way to class one morning, my daughter gave me a drawing to carry with me. But when I uncrumpled it from my bag on the F train, I found a unicorn astronaut, and underneath the words: *when will the unicorn die?* And I cried a little bit behind my mask because not even this immortal creature was going to make it.

I've started filling my apartment with plants because death has been all around us. I favor cacti and succulents because they're hard to kill. At a certain point during the pandemic, my 80-year-old father with cancer got COVID. We brought him to stay with us, monitoring his oxygen levels, ready to zoom to the hospital at any hour. Luckily, he made it through reasonably intact. I, on the other hand, am still in pieces that sailors keep finding all over different parts of the world.

While my father was living on the lower floor of the duplex we watched many old movies, including his favorite, Fellini's *8 ½*, laughed at W.C. Fields, and talked about all the epics we love, including *The Odyssey* and *Ulysses*. I'm Stephen Dedalus and he's Leopold Bloom in our little COVID-induced fever fantasy in which we matter enough to be cast as Dedalus and Bloom. I'm traveling a Dublin transposed onto modern-day Brooklyn, having Joycean epiphanies about art and culture, a son crisscrossing my father in the city streets until we start to form new literary-urban geometries, lurid urban landscapes. Also, he uses the outhouse and feeds the cat. Most of all, I must keep him alive.

In my living room, I have a pink-framed photograph of Anita Ekberg dancing in the fountain in the Fellini movie *La Dolce Vita*, the sweet life. In it, she resembles all the women we've ever used as symbols of sex, death, and some even more intense understanding of life that comes out of the combination of the two. Someone fancy put the photograph out on their Park Slope stoop, and I scooped it up. One person's trash is another person's ode to their wannabe-filmmaker father, his Fellini obsession, and the unthinkable nature of existence that's at once sexy and frankly hard to swallow.

During this surreal and seemingly endless stretch of days in which I ferried between my father and the kids, my daughter asked over and over if he was going to die, if the *wirus* was going to kill him. I told her we were working very hard to prevent that. She asked if I'd tell her if he was dying so she could give him a picture to take with him.

I remember how my father sobbed when he lowered my childhood cat Buttermilk into the earth. He told her goodbye, his face unrecognizable, and called her his good girl. He hoped for her that she was headed somewhere wonderful. I now hope that for him, and for us all.

26. A Small Book of Wanderings, Animals

How else did I survive the pandemic? In part, through reading writers who grappled with complex realities, whose writing styles were as impossible to categorize as my complex new reality. Instead of the snappy odes to Freytag's Pyramid my then-agent recommended so I could sell the novel I was working on that featured a sick father, I started reading writers who also got abducted by their own thought processes. Kate Zambreno: *The publishing people told me that I was writing a novel, but I was unsure. What I didn't tell them is that what I longed to write was a small book of wanderings, animals.*

My agent recommended taking out of my novel all poetic parts and showing instead of telling. I teach craft classes and I get it, but maybe a little telling is good. What's this tyranny of showing? Could it be that telling has been labeled feminine and showing masculine in this context? Every craft book says *show, don't tell,* but some writers say it with more panache than others. Anton Chekhov writes, *Don't tell me the moon is shining; show me the glint of light on broken glass.* Stephen King phrases it like so: *Making people believe the unbelievable is no trick; it's work…Belief and reader absorption come in the details: An overturned tricycle in the gutter of an abandoned neighborhood can stand for everything.*

Trouble is I always lapse into poetry despite my attempt at perfectly sterile smelling prose that says: *you can buy my book; it won't bite; I'm a winner.* But I want to write a book where I glow in a strange way that seems mystical at first but indicates I'm about to burst into flames. And then I do.

I also watched movies that didn't help one iota in the sterile smelling prose department, in the tamping it down and obeying Freytag project. Director Charlie Kaufman tried to do with a *New Yorker* orchid piece by Susan Orlean what I'm trying to do with my city and life. Kaufman's *Adaptation* remains probably my favorite movie about the creative process. His solution is not to follow the lines of nonfiction at all. He features his own struggle to find the story as the central character, and then spikes the ending into a knowingly absurd conflict, throwing in all the other stuff that blockbuster movies must in order to do two things: to make it entertaining, yes, but also to comment on the need to do so, on the sorts of things that grab national attention as entertainment forms, basically because of what our country finds engaging in late Capitalism—gory, franchisable sex and violence between superheroes with fast cuts in expensive-looking locales with strategic product placement. Or something like that. But also to find an ending, which is famously hard to do.

Fiction is difficult for me. I initially stumbled into poetry as a dyslexic child who struggled with the rules of language. For once, I didn't have to worry about my grammar and syntax being "correct." Instead, poetry opened a literary geography of sentence fragments and dangling participles. My early linguistic challenges and consequent turn to poetry caused me to focus on experimentation and I developed an instinct to play with the trappings of various genres, inventing new ones or, in the case of my poet's novel years later, coming at one genre with the tools of another. So what to call what I'm doing here? Textual onanism?

My agent was in the sunset of his life and one day I called him to check in on the novel submission process and he didn't remember who I was. It was a great metaphor for my literary career to date. And then, get this, after my book obviously didn't sell with the agent, the independent press editor who did take it asked if I could put back in all the poetic bits that had been cut for supposed commercial consumption. If that's not a publishing parable, I don't know what is.

At one point, I was reading a chapter from my novel in progress to my mom. I thought my son (who was playing video games, which usually renders him dead to the world), would not listen or care. But it turned out that he had strong opinions on my fictional worldbuilding. He'd been doing a Fiction Writing unit in his amazing public school. He ran out and got his folder with its laminated learning cards and did a long lecture on the various ways I could tweak my character development, setting, problem and solution, author point of view, building of suspense, adding and punctuating dialogue, word choice, and transitions. He covered the pages I'd printed out in red markings (just like Ms. Friedman) that cracked up my mother, and offered to get me started, as his teacher did, by making me fiction task cards, an anchor chart, and a detailed rubric. How could I refuse? The funniest part is that I do believe he made my writing better for this one reason: who has a better bullshit radar than a child? He did have, he added, capping his read pen, one note in particular that was more specific: *A girl named Dylan would never wear purple,* he declared. And out went that storyline.

27. A Friend of Cab Drivers

I asked my son if he wanted to give me another tutorial on this book, but he was trying to raise his Chess Kid puzzle rating, so I picked up poet Ben Lerner's novel *10:04* as a way of thinking about what I wanted to do here. Lerner opens his book walking the High Line after eating baby octopus. In a move that previews the cerebral fireworks to come, as he considers the complexity of octopus life, in a seriocomic manner, he senses an extraterrestrial consciousness, a sensibility that isn't his alone—octopus death and life, and through it a different way of encountering human life. He tells his agent this and they laugh it off. This agent wants him to convert one of his *New Yorker* pieces (another Kaufmanesque act of adaptation) into a novel. But when she asks him how he'll do it, he says: *I'll project myself into several futures simultaneously...I'll work my way from irony to sincerity in the sinking city, a would-be Whitman of the vulnerable grid.* (What he's describing is also another form of descending helix essay but more on this later.) Reading Lerner, I realized that at least part of what the supposed "poet's novel" does is reinvent notions of time and space.

Like Lerner, like me, both *would-be Whitman[s]*, wannabe Whitmans, Whitman himself felt *possess'd at the age of thirty-one to thirty-three, with a special desire and conviction...a feeling or ambition to articulate and faithfully express in literary or poetic form, and uncompromisingly, my own physical, emotional, moral, intellectual, and aesthetic Personality, in the midst of, and tallying, the momentous spirit and facts of its immediate days, and of current America,* and this resulted in *Leaves of Grass,* which he printed at the Rome Brothers Print Shop at Cranberry and Fulton right here in Brooklyn. Not too far from my college, which I do believe somehow is going to make it. This is the college that also gave me my first adjuncting job, before I even had my PhD, so the first place I ever taught at the college level. Then they hired me for this tenure-track position years later, in large part due to the efforts of my professor friend, who enjoys writing about, and writing in, diners (but more on that later, too). The school champions underrepresented students year after year, the ones who stay to chat about Jamaica Kincaid with me for an hour after class. So, basically, if anyone wants to mess with this college, they'll have to go through me first.

Even Whitman, that writer who has become synonymous with poetry, penned two novels, and pondered writing *Leaves of Grass* in other genres, including fiction. He fantasized in his journal about mixing forms so that the stage directions of his imagined play could appear as poetry. His musings reflect the plight of all writers: dreaming of transcending language altogether, giving readers an experience so complete it's not of words at all, much less limited by any one genre. Admittedly, this is an impossible dream. But I suspect the best version of the "poet's novel" takes a new step along the path toward expanding the concept of genre, forging a new form altogether.

Poet James Russell Lowell wrote Whitman off as *a rowdy, a New York tough, a loafer, a frequenter of low places, a friend of cab drivers!* But how is that at all an insult? Please only call me a friend of cab drivers. But this grittiness reflected Whitman's connection to an actual city that many highfalutin writers couldn't really access. As Henry Miller wrote, *in the street you learn what human beings really are; otherwise, or afterwards, you invent them. What is not in the open street is false, derived, that is to say, literature.*

Maybe this is why my kids love to drag junk home from the sidewalk to make sculptures. Is this their version of Miller's street wisdom? My house has become the local dump, housing any number of disowned appliances and dismembered tchotchkes at any given time. But it all becomes worth it when I emerge from my room in the morning to find a rendition of our little family formed entirely out of carved pumpkins and popsicle sticks, and I laugh but in that way where if the world were to end right now, it all would have been enough.

28. Feeding Blood to Ghosts

Now out of the bathroom and dressed, I'm ready to drop the kids, then take the train to my first mammogram (ahoy, middle age), and then to teach at the college. This is when I realize neither of the kids have showered, so I apply some perfume to both. Add a spritz of Febreze just in case.

No matter how overcrowded and malodorous, I cherish Miller's idea of "street" knowledge, starting with my daily commute. As we walk, there's often this teenager swinging by himself in the playground across the street. I have so many questions for him. I'll bet he has all the answers.

The weather is sunny, so I walk them to school instead of taking the subway one stop to Church Avenue. If we go down Greenwood to Macdonald, we can catch a glimpse of our beloved Greenwood Cemetery, which is chock-full of angels and other haunting grave ornaments that my kids like to photograph, but mostly because it's the only time I let them hold my iPhone.

I often think about the childhood directive to hold your breath when you pass a graveyard as I walk by. I've heard it's to avoid making the dead jealous of our ability to breathe but also so spirits don't zoom in. As a child, I kept to this, dutifully holding in the air, cheeks blowfished until it hurt, then that rush when I finally gasp the air back.

But now that I'm older, as I march by this gorgeous graveyard with my kids on the way to school, I breathe in deeply. I realize by now that if the spirits want in badly enough, there's nothing we can do to keep them out. Beside one of the graves this morning stands Goblin. She blows me a fiery kiss and tells me to get ready.

29. Pulling a Dr. Frankenstein

I've seen so many horrors committed by the living at this point that I no longer fear the dead. Too many atrocities committed by the "good guys," so now I've joined Team Deceased. These are now my people. Goblin is their queen. I welcome them inside and cook them dinner. As they eat, various foods can be seen roiling around their transparencies. They hide nothing from me. Yesterday they told me that every time humans pass the graveyard, they, the undead, carefully hold their breath. They want nothing to do with us. And who can blame them?

We pass Foodtown where a babysitter once lost my son when he was three (which may be part of why I've hazarded so few babysitters). I looked for him all over the neighborhood only to find him waiting for me on my stoop, having walked home by himself, wondering what took me so long. He has a sense of direction I'll never comprehend, a spatial comfort in the world that baffles me, as when he'll point out which window is ours from the street in an enormous hotel, while I still regularly get lost in my own neighborhood.

I drop my son at the upper school. On the way to drop my daughter at the lower school, I buy an unreasonably delicious tamale from the guy who sells them out of a cooler, thank him too many times to the point where we're both embarrassed, eat while walking, tamale juice streaming down my chin that I don't wipe away. Then

I shuffle down the subway steps, reaching twice for my kids' hands before remembering they're no longer there, just the spirits of them.

Although it's unthinkable, I think at least once a day of what I'd do if I lost them. I'm certain I'd end up pulling a Dr. Frankenstein, building replicas of them from whatever scraps I could find, maybe even from the manifold unsettling creations they've built all around my house. I'd tuck these garbage sculptures into bed each night until someone pried them from my cold dead hands. Isn't that a fun thought?

As I get closer, I can smell the dark breath of the subway. And yes, the rumors are true. It's our only modern-day underworld, and I have often been Odysseus descending to gain insight. I start with the specter of Teiresias, the seer who has known life as both man and woman, therefore wisest of all. He tells me how to return home but also about the suffering that will come with the journey. Then my mother drinks the blood and can finally see me. When Stephen's mother comes to him as a ghost in the first scene of Joyce's *Ulysses*, he begs her to let him live. Later in the book, Leo Bloom tools around Dublin graveyards and funeral processions, pondering his dead son, father, all those who used to be among us but are no longer. I'm heartbroken by the loss implicit in life but hope I can be more expansive if I learn to breathe it in.

30. Unreal Land, Possibly Nonexistent

Inside the station, I gape at the posters as I pass, always marveling at the ones where the women's (it's always the women's) faces are altered in disturbing ways with markers, things are taken away such as teeth, or added, such as dicks sticking out of their mouths, and I worry about all of our futures.

The parrot on the guy's shoulder on the F train tells me to go check myself, so it's already a very Brooklyn morning. I try to make a clever retort, but the man tells me the parrot is shy. The high school girls dress just like we did. There's one across from me who looks so much like I did, wearing just what I did and reading *The Invisible Man*. She's wearing baggy jeans, a faded Tom Waits T-shirt and Converse; her hair is gathered into two buns atop her head that resemble the beginnings of horns. I long to reach out and touch them, but I control myself.

It's like a Brooklyn subway time warp. We lock eyes and I wonder if she knows this is what she'll look like in the future. I almost want to ask her if she has any questions for her future self, as I had so very many. But I don't want to spoil the fun of her finding it all out, each twist ending and cliffhanger, all the way to the inevitable denouement.

The a.m. rush of being overcaffeinated and feeling my brain start to flicker, that restless firefly stuck in this city, in this ghost story nation, haunted by American history. I finish all grading and lesson planning on the Harlem Renaissance and its Descendants while standing up and winding my body around the subway pole. There I attempt to write any pages of this book in the notes section of my iPhone with shaking hands, which I accidentally erase when I get a seat, and flash-fall asleep on a very understanding older bearded man's shoulder. He smells like weed and forbearance. He says, *looks like you fell asleep for a second there, kiddo,* and I want to stay forever.

Which is to say: here I am on the subway to work again, emitting text from my pores, shooting it out of embarrassing orifices, and then seeking to shape that amber liquid into something legible to my fellow straphangers. Trouble is I don't have the faintest idea how to structure it. But since it came from my body, I decide to give it tendons instead of grammar. I wouldn't be sure where to shelve it, though, nor do I think I need to be anymore after living, like everyone else, through years of rampant instability and plagues both literal and figurative.

Ralph Foster Weld called Brooklyn *a vague and unreal land, possibly nonexistent,* and this is one thousand percent true. Throw out a street name and I'll tell you something surreal that happened to me there, the smell of pickles and their brine somehow always on the wind. As I am of Brooklyn, that *friend of cab drivers,* Whitman was also a fanboy. He made no secret of his love for this borough. Here he is nailing the Brooklyn writer *forever mood: I too lived, Brooklyn of ample hills was mine, / I too walk'd the streets of Manhattan island, and bathed in the waters around it, / I too felt the curious abrupt questionings stir within me, / In the day among crowds of people sometimes they came upon me.*

I know nothing of prairies, but the urban sublime is that instant when we break out of the tunnels and are briefly sun-blinded. It's everything. Times are bleak but at least the subway pulls out of the ground long enough for a quickie epiphany. As the woman across from me touches her earlobe three times in a row, I think how if I loved her, that's the gesture I would love best. This very pale high school boy, with reddish lips and night-colored hair is scratching his neck with a pen as he reads *Twilight*, and I consider what I will do if he turns out to be a literal vampire. Probably let him bite me. I wonder if the abundance of sun hurts him.

He's leaning the *Twilight* book on his enormous backpack, and I mentally frame it. When he looks up, he catches me staring at him and holds my eye for a second longer than is polite, and I feel for one subway clanking second that we've known each other forever, that maybe I'm his familiar, in the vampire sense, gifted with one iota of his vampiric powers.

On the way to work, here I am, abruptly, powerfully, connected to everyone on that train, our shared personhood echoing through the tunnels we've just exceeded. Aside from the vampire guy, what am I thinking about? How my mom thinks the lyrics to Elton John's *Tiny Dancer* involve Tony Danza, and how when she sings them in her croaky man-voice I like her so much I could explode. Then right after the Elton-Tony interlude, we bust out of the earth at Fourth Avenue and Ninth. All my formative experiences prismed back to me in that hot second when we erupt from tunnel to luminescence. Not too shabby for a Monday.

31. Uncharted Lands

As we break into the light, that little girl tracing the train window with her lollipop illuminates in a flash. How the parent in me feels I should tell her not to put it back in her mouth as it's now soot-covered (her own father does so) but the other part of me wants to say, *take this magic wand and write your future in soot on the window, then crack it, and run away; they'll only domesticate you.* I don't say this, but I do grin too widely at her in a manner that must look frightening since she hides behind her dad. The vampire gets off at Carol Street and I miss his vampiric possibilities already.

The whippersnappers are still subway surfing I discover while watching the girl I thought of as teenage me scramble aboard. The freedom. The risk. The youth of it. There's a part of me that wants to join her, invite the vampire along, surf those tunnels like something paranormal with absolutely nothing to lose. It reminds me how so many stories are about older folks revisiting the spaces of their more vital younger selves, but I just want to hold on, to never let her go, or be the ghost that haunts her, that yanks her forward into 2023, says, *surprise, would you just look at these jowls?!* I'll tell her, *one day you'll have to pluck about one chin hair a month. Yes, chin hair. You'll have no idea what they are doing there. You will feel guilty uprooting them as they are something trapped in your aging flesh but dreaming of the eternal, just like you.*

People cleverer than I have written about that literary twist where the city turns out to be the book's main character, and they're not wrong. New York, you've been everything to me, your trains cutting through subway tracks my only way of making sense of the world. Sometimes I even catch myself imagining my own insides according to your radical structures, especially since car metaphors are lost on me. Even my use of language feels stolen from the rhythms of your twisting, often broken, subway cars flashing through darkened uncharted lands.

You may have to run for the G train every time (why?! citywide prank? behavioral experiment?) but when you rise over the Gowanus Canal and glimpse the Statue of Liberty it's all worth it. There's always construction there. What have they been building all this time? Another Gowanus Canal under the current one? So it can have a doppelgänger? And how do I visit it? What else could it be? Aside from the mind, what sort of structure involves infinite becoming? If we follow this logic, have they been building a brain under the Gowanus Canal all along? If so, why wasn't I notified? It's right up my alley. I suspect we would have smelled it though. I wonder about the odor of our brains: so many thoughts in such close quarters. If I ever discover what they're making, I'll let you know. Unless it's condominiums.

I pull out a book and then, I kid you not, while reading *10:04,* there Ben Lerner is, with his daughters. That's the thing about living in Brooklyn. I'm sitting across from him, reading his book, feeling haunted in a good way by this author and the structure of his work. Then, poof, there he is, sitting right there, like I've manifested him by crushing so hard on his words. A father reading to his children on the train. Since I picture subways as zooming through our shared brain networks, and all that goes on there as a form of writing, this instant casts the two of us as characters in the larger book that is Brooklyn. And is it just my imagination, or does he catch sight of his book in my hand, resulting in one brief, blushing instant of recognition?

32. Ben Lerner Separation Anxiety

If I catch the F, I get off at Jay Street Metrotech, and if it's the G, Hoyt. On this day of Ben Lerner, it's Jay Street, which is closer to the imaging place. I'm nervous, but the woman giving me my first mammogram is so sweet, I keep saying over and over *I appreciate you* as she refers to my breasts as *girls,* puts weird stickers on them, and contorts me to take pictures of my insides. As this happens, I see the before and after of middle age, my body starting to be something that might fall apart any time now.

Afterwards, the nice lady and I look at images of the insides of my breasts together like old friends, as though we're trying to communicate with something deep in my body, perhaps even early signals of my future death. I have this startling realization, standing there, as she exudes warmth, that this is the fetus version of what my dad is having to do post-cancer diagnosis: I must start letting go of my body, my sense of ownership and control over it, its health, its ability to please anyone but me, and eventually its time here on an embattled earth that's lately more of a hellscape. The first half of my life was for getting a good grip and the second is an elongated form of loosening. I'm walking off into the sunset over here. But first I need a coffee.

After the mammogram, I walk out of my way because a good cup of coffee is worth any detour. If I go that route, I can see both my coffee cart guy and my lady justice on top of the courthouse, both minor deities. I remind myself every time I pass to look up her history. But at the same time, I don't want her to become an academic interest like everything else in my life, so I leave her some mystery. But of course I don't really. Instead, I Google her as I walk, almost falling in front of her court building as I discover she's Themis, Greek goddess of wisdom, justice, interpreter of the will of the gods, the lady with all the answers, once the owner of the oracle of Delphi before gifting it to Apollo. What's more, in the *Cypria*, she's the one who works with Zeus to plan the Trojan War. Why? Overpopulation.

As I look up at her, I ponder the emphasis on balance she calls to mind with her scales, and I notice she also has a sword. It fits the current cultural climate. While my daughter tried to braid the scallions this morning, I'd read an article on how to teach students critical thinking when our country is so polarized. But it's hard when anyone with a different opinion wants to skin you with a hot bayonet, have you drawn and quartered, or witness your hanging in the town square.

I buy the huge coffee from the ancient coffee cart guy, Hector, who tells me jokes, and whom I love like my own father. Hector is so humble that he never mentions how he's the greatest warrior fighting for Troy in the Trojan War. I've asked him and he's not a fan of Homer. I don't bring up Themis since she's responsible in one text for his having to fight in the first place.

Hector is a jokester. This morning, as I'm rifling through my bag to find my wallet, he says, *quick, how did the hipster burn his tongue?* I ask, *how?* while unearthing a diaper my daughter hasn't needed in years from my bag. Hector says, *he drank his coffee before it was cool.*

I laugh way too loudly, pay, and start to walk away, while removing the green Health Bar (what even is that?) from my enormous Mary Poppins sack that contains everything in the universe. I open, sniff, put this bar back in the sack immediately, and walk backwards towards Hector, who holds out the huge, pink, sprinkly donut he knows I wanted all along. Because we are spiritually bound. He says, *may today bring you happiness*, and I am now planning our wedding in my head, even though he's about forty years older than me and doesn't dig Homer.

Next, I pass the Brooklyn Tabernacle, which blasts choir music that I actually enjoy in the morning—despite being raised a heathen—especially when I'm feeling cranky. Maybe the bad mood is mammogram-related or even due to Ben Lerner separation anxiety. Or the sinking sensation that I'll never write anything as good as *10:04*. But remembering Hector's wish for my happiness does help. That and the choir music. I wonder if it can bless me if I'm not religious. I hope so.

33. Fries and Good Diner Coffee

Next, I walk by the New Apollo Diner. The tale of my professor friend (from earlier), another parable: after being placed away from his department as "not a Senior Lecturer," he took his name plate and set up office in this very same diner. He now produces his wonderful creative writing, which often features diners, and meets with students over fries and good diner coffee. The moral? You often need to pitch your own literary/academic tent. You can't wait for someone else to do it for you. Getting people to visit is another question. But I'll obviously come. I never say no to fries and good diner coffee.

I stop to get flowers to put on the desk of my fries and good diner coffee professor friend because we just did a reading together where he, as they say, rocked it. I also want to thank him too late for the job I may be about to lose. When I enter the flower shop, there's a piece of fecal matter on the floor. The people who work there are gathered around it. As I get closer, one of them is saying, *what I really need to know is whether what we're dealing with here comes from a dog or from a human because that will greatly influence how I react here.*

As though it had been waiting in the wings to make its grand entrance, a tiny white dog runs across the carpet tiles. *I told you not to bring that mutt in, Rita,* says the lady behind the register. They dispose of the dog's business. We cackle together at this bizarre shard of shared experience. But the whole scenario really literalizes what we're all afraid of, what the woman behind the counter says: *See? This city is going to shit.* I retain hope, though, because that's just one more of my annoying habits. I'm Sunny, the optimistic pony, even if it makes you want to punch me in the face.

Faced with what looks like a posse of yellow-lashed, all-seeing eyes, I decide to go with the sunflowers. As I tell the lady, I nod in their direction, but refuse to return the flowers' naked stare. If I were to make eye contact, I decide for some strange reason, they'd immediately glean everything about me, and I'm not cool with that. Why do I always long to be at once seen and invisible? *Thank you,* I say, holding the paper-wrapped blooms to my chest as I rush back out into downtown Brooklyn.

Soon I get to the college. This is always a peaceful time unless the flasher in the residential building across from us is already awake. Yes, you read that correctly. The flasher could also be glimpsed a floor down in my classroom where I tried to coax 18-year-olds to care about writing at eight thirty in the morning, as they watched TikTok videos of dogs dressed as humans on their laptops while pretending to do in-class essays.

The flasher throws off my day because he is a time machine back to another man who forced his way into my personal space, shall we say, to put it lightly. Every time after I see the flasher, I must waste time calming myself and getting all my body parts to work again. I hate how he causes me to malfunction. I call the guy from the car place on the corner to come and use his cables to jumpstart me. He's always very understanding about it. I decided to get ahead of the whole ChatGPT fiasco and become a machine myself. I figure it would save me a lot more heartbreak down the line.

Before I teach my first class of the day, I pull out a white hair, remove what looks like silly putty (hopefully) from my black shirt, apply more Chapstick and a huge smile; remind myself to do a deep dive into BookTok; attempt to tweet or post something "writerly" to

Instagram; decide it looks self-indulgent; delete it; post it again anyway; delete it.

As I'm about to walk in, my phone rings. I see the number of my daughter's lower school and my heart stops. *What happened to her?* It's the school nurse. She tells me my daughter is fine (phew) but just has a booboo from where she tried to fly. *Tried to fly? Off the desk. Oh.* She puts my daughter on the phone, and her little voice apologizing is too much. *I'm just glad you're okay. No more trying to fly, though. OK?*

Next, I try to teach college students how to fly, no, how to write essays; ask one student to gently poke another one who's snoring loudly at least once; wonder why I do this job at least once. But then the students get it, and it feels like a spotlight comes on in my classroom, and I can hear *The Lion King's* "Circle of Life" playing in my head. Until one of my favorite students, an athlete who recently injured himself and won't be able to continue with his sport, starts crying behind his laptop.

Though the mom part of me badly wants to, I don't hug him because I don't want to get fired or canceled. I approach him with my arms firmly at my sides and tell him I'll help in any way I can, pondering how I could ever possibly aid someone athletically as I say it. We're lucky to have him here, seeing as he's a hilarious class clown in the best possible way, the best student in the class, and a stellar athlete. I decide to hold off on discussing braided essays until everyone can focus because they are my favorite (and I know they will be his)—for the way they interweave any and all seemingly incompatible threads, yielding striking discoveries about reader, writer, world, and all that lies beyond it. They take you down a thought path that seems one way at first but always turns out to be something entirely different, whether it be an overt twist ending, or a more subtle metamorphosis that happens in increments. I wish I could show my crying student how to braid together the various confusing threads of this day he's had in order to find some sort of narrative closure.

Instead of the braided essay lecture followed by a think-pair-share I'd planned this morning while my daughter pretended to be a Bento lunch box, I take the students to the on-campus coffee shop and let them order whatever they want. As we sit in the booths, we switch roles as they educate me about old people technology faux pas and how to avoid them. In case you were wondering, fellow old folks (by which I mean anyone over the age of twenty), yes, a thumbs-up really does come across as passive aggressive in texts.

I do take one opportunity to teach them something because I just can't help myself. I see their texting etiquette hack and raise them a how to email your professor without being one thousand percent rude tutorial. As we stuff donuts in our mouths and guzzle coffee, I ask them to please stop doing things like starting your email to me, as one student did last semester, with *hey honey.* That's a hard no. Though they never take notes, this time they do, and they thank me profusely for the lesson afterwards. I think it's because I prefaced it by promising them these sneaky little strategies (called just not being discourteous) would score them an A from all their professors. I'd said I was kidding after but, judging by the avid notetaking, they may not have heard that part through all the munching. Class time is over, or I'd teach them about the munching too if I could is how much I love teaching.

Visionary though he might have been, Whitman was not in love with teaching the way I am. In the 1830s, when the newspaper business declined as New York City prepared to enter a depression, Whitman turned to pedagogy. *O, damnation, damnation!* he wrote, *thy other name is school-teaching.* Yet, though it can still make me nervous, especially on the first day, to stand before any mass of people, teaching has often been my reason to get up in the morning, as it was today. An extroverted introvert, the figurative spotlight encircling me simultaneously horrifies me and is home. I become a new kind of being under its glow. Sometimes I must put on a second, less skinless self to get out the door so I can attempt to help college students find their voices, but some days include donuts and texting lessons, and then it's all a little easier.

34. Finding Their Voices at Walmart

In my next class, which also has the same student athlete in it, at first the students in the front row aren't paying attention. My bra straps cut into my sweated back. I have poison ivy all over my body from a recent visit to my parents' house, and I'm having full-body itching fantasies as I try to teach them about outlining. I try to convey the mindboggling liberties Ander Monson's piece, *Outline Toward a Theory of the Mine Versus the Mind and the Harvard Outline*, takes with structure, but I can see that I'm losing them and need to recalibrate. My body longs to rise out of its container and soar into the audience, leave them different somehow. Because, like it or not, when we interact with things, we change them.

But then I chill out and start talking rhetorical triangles. We analyze Freytag's pyramid, locate the story phases of a Budweiser commercial, discuss how storytelling relates to business (many of my students are business majors who find my professional life choices questionable at best), and do what I call my *Roshomon* exercise, which is like a more grownup, literary version of playing Telephone. Students interview each other in a group and then tell their own version of each story. The differences are astounding and help highlight complexities of perspective and the role of the narrator in storytelling. For example, am I an unreliable narrator? Who's to say?

Then, most crucially, we discuss how we can take Freytag's pyramid apart and reconstruct or reinvent it. My student-athlete-class-clown asks if he could purchase this new thought structure at Walmart, and I tell him probably, that we'll have to Google it to know for sure. We all laugh but we will all also Google it.

Like most of my classes, this one's full of people who've been told their voices don't matter, who are suddenly finding that they do. They are finding their voices at Walmart. I treasure my student athlete who suggests this dreamlike possibility. When asked to describe themselves in a single word, one student is *syncopated*; another *retro* because he prefers vintage clothing and vinyl; one is *new*, which initially sounds conventional, except he organizes his thoughts around his mother's horrible cooking, which drives his family to new galaxies of culinary adventure as a workaround—now that's innovation; one describes himself as *lost*, which he's wise to have figured out so early in life since so much of living is just variations of this state; and my class clown is *displaced* because his family had been forced to move around, while he was a baby, during Hurricane Katrina—which another student pointed out was just a headline to the rest of them.

But later, my student's joke takes on more dimension when he shares that Walmart had provided help during Katrina before government agencies could get in there. And yet again writing, and the brainstorming that goes into it, becomes a record of what has reached in and touched our lives at various points, eventually forming a grove of letters others can navigate.

35. Mental Sparkle

I try to cheer my students up in this dark time, teaching youth activism-themed composition courses, with such utopian titles as *Writing to Change the World* and screening that documentary about the organization that turns guns into shovels to plant trees. All I can hope is that these things inspire students to make a difference in this cracked world. I like to think that as I teach, we form some sort of conceptual bridge, a piece of me transmigrates into my students, a piece of them into me. But mostly they play on their cell phones while I wax poetic about the college essay.

But it's impossible to be entirely cheerful with all that's going down. We read Raven Leilani's short story "Breathing Exercise" alongside such realities as Eric Garner's saying eleven times that he couldn't breathe. George Floyd's loss of breath hadn't happened yet when Leilani published the story, but it has happened in our world, so we talk about that. My displaced-class clown-student athlete asks how he can love a world that doesn't love his people back and says the feeling of wool in the lungs from Leilani's story sounds familiar. I don't have a pithy response, but we will come at this question from various angles over the semester together. It's the best we can do. When we discuss Claudia Rankine's "The Condition of Black Life Is One of Mourning" and I ask students to come up with plans to improve our society by way of legislation, that same student suggests the only legislative solution would be a time machine.

In *The Black Period*, which we read an excerpt from this morning, Hafizah Augustus Geter writes, *taking my cue from art, I named what I had lost what I was attempting to remake: the Black Period.* One student describes the sensation she's left with after this reading as a state of "mental sparkle." After reading Geter, my students want to rewrite their own cultural landscapes, write themselves into a society that hasn't featured them in the first place. As a white lady professor, I can't tell them I totally understand. But I can present them with as many ways into the questions they have as possible. I can share with them texts that gift them this mental sparkle, and provide them with rewriting tools and ways in. We can find our voices at Walmart, learn together how to look closely at what has been in order to reimagine what could be, as I hope all my gutsy future leaders-in-training will do.

36. Take it in Blood

My students laugh when I call them future leaders, but I've been teaching long enough to see this transformation: how shaky college presentations can show me some flashing image of how they will speak to crowds in the coming years. I wish I could explain to them how the mind has folds, and when you're in one it's so hard to see beyond to the next. But one day everything can change. When they tell me they are terrible presenters, I tell them I'll be first in line at their future book signings.

All this doesn't change the fact that there are students lined up to cry in my office after class because COVID, long hours at jobs, raising kids while going to school, because racism, because sexism, because depression, because they lost their athletics, because they fear the college is about to shut down. It doesn't change the fact that I will wait until they leave and then cry in that same office because I can't seem to stop absorbing other people's feelings. I was born without an epidermis or a dermis and there was nothing the doctors could do about it. All I can do is receive them, listen, and sometimes feed them sweets because I am the creepy goblin who lives in the academic woods. Just a reminder that your college students are holding themselves together with tape through such challenges as just generally being alive right now, so don't forget to bring treats. After that second class, I lock myself in the office and eat all the leftover donuts, chug cold coffee, and blast Lou Reed's "Vicious" until I feel ready to go about my day.

Luckily, there are brighter days. After my students said they hated poetry, I played them Jay-Z - rap as poetry - and gave them an excerpt from the lyrics to Nas's "Take it in Blood" to analyze, and am now fielding emails from students about how they can get into the poetry scene. Clearly, my work here is done. *Mic drop*

There are also the hilarious teacher moments when you really see that your students are from a different generation. After class, and before I cry and eat the donuts while playing Lou Reed, my student who made the Walmart joke walks back with me to my office.

I have a photo of a young Bob Dylan on my desk, and he asks if this is...my husband. But it's Bob Dylan. And the laugh we share when I explain to him who Bob Dylan is, gets both of us through the day. I remind him how Jay-Z said musician Dylan gets mentioned as one of the best writers of all time but what about Biggie? And now he remembers Dylan.

I'm working so hard to build these creative communities for young people as the world burns to a crisp. Sometimes I imagine all of us holding hands as our bodies become vegetation that heals our effed-up earth. It's a tall order, I know. I never said I wasn't dramatic. Okay, so I can't fix this broken world, but I can tell students how to transform their brains into secret gardens by employing Ray Bradbury's reading method, which I try to do as often as I can: One poem a night, one short story a night, one essay a night, for the next thousand nights. For me, tonight will be Carmen Maria Machado's "The Husband Stitch," Elizabeth Acevedo's "Ode to the Head Nod," and Jimmy Santiago Baca's "Coming into Language." It will be the best night ever.

37. Language is Nakedness

Solid proof that the universe has a sick sense of humor: I'm in the next class, in the middle of telling my students about self-exposure in memoir, when one of them points out the flasher across the way. I want to tell this exhibitionist, *you can't scare me with that; I've mothered myself through childhood trauma and peak-pandemic times with two kids, a new job, and no childcare. You want a fright? You should see post-COVID college enrollment and morale. You want a fright? Try being a woman in a country where 21 South Carolina politicians just proposed the death penalty for women who have abortions.*

In the apartment above the flasher, there stands Goblin. She's outsized and growing bigger by the minute. Her furred paws are smashing the windows above the flasher's apartment. She holds up a lighter and threatens to set the building aflame. I can tell by this that she wants me to stand up for myself. But I just shake my head. Goblin stops smashing windows. She stares back at me with a mixture of anger and disappointment that withers me.

I don't say or do anything because the flasher can't even hear me all the way over here, and because I'm too chickenshit. Instead, I go back to showing the students how to document ephemera. I tell myself that next time I will act. Goblin wags her furry black finger, drops the lighter and pads away.

I check in with the students to make sure they're all okay after the whole flasher incident. They're all laughing about it, so I assume so. But it's hard to tell so I remind them that I'm here if they need to talk. But what I really should have done is fly, as my daughter tried to do, over the expanse between the buildings and given him the old what for.

Instead, after class I tear up in the bathroom stall and then try to fix it with Visine. When I look at myself in the mirror afterward, it's not good. There's this Amy Schumer sketch in which three actresses, Tina Fey, Julia Louis-Dreyfus and Patricia Arquette, sit around a table and discuss their *last fuckable moment*. They conclude it's forty. Part of me can't wait to become an old witch out in a fairytale cabin in the woods, just sending passive aggressive thumbs-up texts to everyone and emails to all my old professors that begin, *hey honey*. I'll be post-etiquette.

But the other part of me has lived as a "woman" (whatever the eff that is), with my currency being measured, like a cartoon thermometer I can watch rising and falling, by what others think of my appearance. Such a huge part of the shock of aging is learning how to navigate a world that has been unsafe because certain people wanted to fuck you, but soon nobody will want to fuck you anymore.

I'm going to really have fun with it. I'm not talking junior league stuff either. Forget this not shaving business. I mean, obviously I won't shave. But I'm thinking bigger, like growing my fingernails long enough to curl and pop the multiverse. When nobody wants me, I wonder if I'll finally be free, transmogrify into a wizened, sexless paranormal entity or merely become invisible, just *presto change-o*, into the Nether. I want to rewrite all of it: not have to be the object of that stale old tale but rather the architect of a whole new city of women valued only for their wilds inside.

38. Eating Flamin' Hot Cheetos Naked in Bed

What if, as I age, my skin parts and a different organism entirely has space to emerge? Something sharp and thrilling? It would usher in a whole new possible way to live that requires not clinging to the devastation of the old but becoming something entirely new, a third thing maybe. A hag brilliance. All the old fear and limits falling away in favor of creativity, ferocity, and writing in my diary all day until the pages bleed, while eating Flamin' Hot Cheetos naked in bed, a beer bottle cap stuck to my forehead that resembles the beginning of a horn. Goblin mode.

But I'm still one foot in the old world and one foot in the new. Or at least that's what I fantasize as I witness the small wreckage of my face each morning and still employ the futility that is wrinkle cream. I hope to one day make performance art of my changing visage, to dig deeper ruts in my face that you can journey through until you're close enough to peer inside my brain. Surprise: there are more goblins there. That's when the fun will really begin.

As I think back on the flasher, I envision using one of my future-curled-fingernails as a weapon against him. At the same time, I have a strange thought, and maybe it's more of a making lemonade from penis-bearing lemons sort of vibe. But I part the anger to wonder if I would have ended up as the writer I am (gauche, disgusting, but honest about some things that go unsaid, maybe for good reason, *hey honey)* if I hadn't been shoved face-to-face with strangers all the time, lured into imagining in stunning detail their daily lives—even this flasher's? For instance, why does he do it? Is he so lonely and detached from anything human that his only form of language is nakedness?

39. Speculative Maps

Here's the crazy thing: some girls grow up with the sound of cicadas instead of sirens, in *Gilmore Girls*-like villages with gazebos adorned in Christmas lights, without men thrusting their junk in their faces or whacking off on trains whenever they turn around. I started taking the subway to school in fifth grade and many of these men probably had daughters my age. How did they separate the precious daughters they were meant to protect from me? All those errant members popping up all over the place must've had some effect on how my brain developed. I live in a permanent state of emergency or maybe it's more precise and scientific to call it penis brain. All I can hope is that urban overstimulation also results in heightened states of inspiration and good prose, but perhaps that's sugar-coating it. I think it boils down to: I must tell myself I'm a better writer for having gone through perdition or else I'll explode—and not in a lovely indie film sort of way.

I like to drum up speculative maps of how each part of my (city, too) experience has influenced my thinking. This hypothetical geography helps me process such complexities as trauma and imagination and calms me when the sirens are going off. But, see, there are never not sirens going off. This was doubly true during peak-COVID. But I will also never forget the sound of people opening their windows at seven every evening, banging pots and pans and making other forms of music, to come together and thank the frontline workers. This was also the time each day that I would journey through Brooklyn with my kids to look at the rainbows other children had put up in their windows, as a way of making contact. Did you know that they have already started archiving those rainbows as historical relics?

I read somewhere that sirens give you that panicky feeling because they're made to sound like crying babies. So, I was reared on the sonics of wailing infants, and was therefore always in training for my current maternal role. I'm not sure what I was training for with random peckers cropping up here and there (stunned exotic dancer?), but let's leave that aside for now. The emergencies and suffering (as well as the private parts) of others are never distant in a city. I sleep partially awake, ready to save my children, the city's children, or my own inner child from any disaster that might crop up—perhaps neither fire nor ice, but an enormous, apocalyptic end-times phallus. Long story short: I'm exhausted; in dog years, I'm dead.

I rarely sleep through the night without a scared kid in my bed, and I missed my last dental appointment because I had to get my son stitches. I need to make an appointment before my teeth rot out of my head and I become not only no longer a youthful woman but a literal Chucky Doll that tries to murder you in your sleep. The dentist will not be possible this week though, especially since it's hard enough to find time to get to the urgent care if my eye is pussing or I can't swallow from the third bout of strep in three months caused by some amalgam of having children as a health risk in general and being a sarcastic woman—because I've heard that's well-worthy of being smote by the ancient patriarchal idea of god.

40. The Skin of Cartoon Extraterrestrials

When I visit my parents, in the place they've moved to since the pandemic (rural traitors), the minute I get there, my blood pressure drops. I smell grass and what can technically be called air, rather than the exhaled hopes and dreams of eight million New Yorkers. I forget my devices, ambitions, and all the ways I'm trying to fill myself up. I sit in the woods with the stink bugs, hoot owls, and moss that looks like the skin of cartoon extraterrestrials. Recently I had students write a pamphlet that tells extraterrestrials how to live a good life on earth, but I wonder if any of us really know.

My kids return to the earth when they visit my parents. They follow neon-green caterpillars on logs for hours, charting their journeys through various panoramas until my dad calls them for dinner. Since my dad got sick, I've become the grill-master. I drizzle the lighter fluid over the coals like a mad scientist, then use a bizarrely long match that my mom hands me to light that whole scene up.

I play soccer with my son and volleyball with my daughter while the various foods burn. After dinner we do bubbles, water balloons, and a game we made up called *wipeout,* which involves lining up pinecones and then knocking them down with sticks that resemble Zeus's lightning bolts. Then, right before bed, we do sparklers, tracing codes of light into the air near the Pine trees. My son sleeps on the carpet in my parents' room with his mouth wide open, and I sleep in the upstairs bed, wearing my daughter as a quilt. She spreads herself over me like we never stopped sharing a body, and I never move her because she did actually used to be part of me, so it feels homey. Plus, one day she'll be a teenager and hate me, so I must soak it all in now. I wrap my arms and legs around her and wake hardly able to walk the next morning but furiously joyful. When my son lies on my stomach, he says he's lying on his *first home*.

There are wild turkeys around my parents' house that gather by the windows. My mother feeds them birdseed, refers to them as her gentlemen callers, and treats them like old-fashioned suitors. I wonder how my father feels about this. I think pretty okay since he comes trotting out whenever she rings her turkey bell. Yes, there's a bell. She sends me daily photos of the birds, and it forms such a contrast to my urban day that I can barely believe we inhabit the same globe.

We're not allowed to move around behind the glass sliding doors when the turkeys are here lest we frighten them, so my son, daughter and I crouch and ogle the absurd birds when they come. I've come to recognize some of them and feel genuinely congratulatory when they emerge with new chicks. The kids name them. I joke that I'll throw them a Turkey-themed baby shower. I'm confident my parents and kids would attend and take it very seriously. I think of the turkeys as my good luck talismans. Because animals are just around to be incorrectly interpreted for human needs, right?

The turkeys were peering into the window behind me as I had my final academic Zoom interview. My kids also ran in various times. At one point, while I shook and tried to impress the search committee for my dream job over Zoom, my son came in to say he was running away because Yaya (what he calls my mom) wouldn't let him play with fire, and then my daughter came in with her face painted like a cat and picked her nose behind me. It was patently ridiculous, and I'm pretty sure it's why I finally got my current job. They were like, *we need to give this woman from the turkey circus a job before she becomes entirely feral and covered in turkeys.* Please don't try to talk sense into me on this one. It's a fool's errand.

41. Figuring Out How to Be a Human

As with my mother and her turkeys, not surprisingly, my father also has manifold eccentricities. Like the rest of us, he's still figuring out how to be a human. My friends were surprised on sleepovers to wake to find him performing his exercise routine that resembles shadow boxing mixed with the Foxtrot, while still wearing the football-style teeth grinding nightguard he finds at the pharmacy next to the compression socks. Sometimes reality doesn't even appear to be believable. He believes in magic as I do, and will do overelaborate rituals if I, say, tell him I have a book on submission, as I do right now.

My parents are nutty to be sure but also often wonderful. I get to see them parenting again, as though I could go back in time and watch them, but this time with my own children. They create worlds for them. My mother carefully invents each year not just an Easter egg hunt, but an Easter egg ecosphere—the baroque candy we can arrange in the basket, the eggs and all the materials to dye them, my father's eggs benedict. It's an egg orgy. And let's not forget the eggy way we all ended up here. It's like, as we both witness and participate in the festivities, we are doing honor to our origins, we are tipping our hats, as we employ the English muffins to sop up the last of the running yolk, to the fact that we all started out as eggs. In many ways I've had two childhoods. This is my second. With my kids. Somehow, both times I found out I was pregnant, I was visiting my mother, making eggs, and they were double-yolked.

When we visit, my mom goes all out, driving to the store weeks ahead of time to gather all the things my kids love to consume or bat around. I feel safe in saying there is no other grandma who can still beat her grandkids in a potato sack race or arm-wrestling match like my tough, wiry mother—more Wyatt Earp than Mrs. Claus. She plays Badminton and Bocce Ball, tramps down the rickety path to the lake with us to spend hours throwing the donut floats to the kids— an exercise in futility, but she doesn't mind. She treats this launching of pastry missiles with the utmost seriousness. She's in the school of putting your all into whatever you do, even if it's chucking floats that resemble frosted desserts. I have inherited this and view nothing as more crucial than the throwing of the donut floats.

As the kids float around, my mom and I sit on the dock together. I tell her about whatever I'm attempting to write, and listen to her long, unhurried, Southern-style tales in which each detail has a starring role. Her stories snake through my consciousness for days after as I try to figure out what the hidden message was. Trying to find the thesis statement, as I say to my students. There's always a hidden message, making my mom one of the more intriguing codes to crack. Then it hits me: the why of her seemingly pointless story, and it's often profound, sneakily so.

Next, I tell her about whatever I'm reading, and she provides her twisty, hard-to-follow yet oddly right-on take on whatever it is. She liberally throws in asides, non sequiturs, and off-kilter quips that she refers to as evidence of her *British sense of humor*. Nobody in the family is sure what makes her sense of humor *British*. Satire of an absurd universe?

Sometimes we hold hands, as I remember, as my kids remind me, how her body used to be my condominium. When my daughter inevitably creates an enigmatic collection of lake oddities around my mom that soak and dirty us, my mother takes the swamp assemblage seriously as art, which makes my daughter light up the lake around her with little girl pride. Mom points out how the way my daughter has arranged it makes the seaweed resemble a dragon, and my daughter nods wisely. And here's where I remember how Mom carefully wrote down my poems as a kid like they mattered.

42. Inhaling Spirits at Cemeteries

At one point during the pandemic, while my parents were visiting still-more elderly family to make sure they were okay, my kids and I got an Airbnb outside the city to hear ourselves think. We didn't want to be like all the others who'd permanently abandoned the streets of Brooklyn, with their odors of summer-cooked garbage, but we needed a minute to discover grasshoppers on a leaf. There were bullfrogs in an abandoned pool next to the house. At night they were deafening in a way that reminded me of all living things that had come before. We went to our first Renaissance fair, saw people make Medieval puns, swallow fire, and act like life-size chess pieces, which particularly thrilled my chess-obsessed son. We had found our people. We were walking through history, lumbering through Medieval times, living time out of order, in the midst of a Renaissance, a rebirth.

My daughter (and I) of course became infatuated with the fire-swallowing lady who also walked on glass. She said this is what she wanted to do when she grew up. She wanted to know how this woman could do all these things without pain. My son explained to her that either she was faking it, or she was a sorceress. Not surprisingly, my daughter preferred the sorceress option. My son enjoyed the Renaissance fair but missed the wild turkeys. Fair enough.

But, even though it doesn't have fire-swallowers (on my block at least) or wild turkeys, there's still something moving about being in Brooklyn, where parents cart kids around in baskets on the back of bikes. I absorb Brooklyn's rhythms and shoot them out as lines on paper that reflect the structure and beat of the city. Like, let me just tell you about right now. I'm sitting in my office at work after the whole flasher incident. Since we moved to the new campus, it's now a mass of cubicles, but I can still see the sky, so I'm good. I'm drinking my now-cold coffee, using my office computer but not for office stuff, to write to you, which feels at least minimally illicit, letting all the noise in my brain finally drain out into the white expanse of this Word document. It's paradise. But I'm not happy with most of what I write, so I delete it. I leave the part about my brain draining and paradise to remember how I was once happy in case it never happens again.

Since I'm a drama queen and overly sensitive to any change that makes my mind move differently, I must visualize all sorts of things to avoid getting pulled into a maelstrom of past-regurgitated trauma after seeing the flasher. I scroll through pictures of my kids pretending to be statues this morning to cheer myself up. My son's friend has a phone, so I sometimes receive texts from my son during the school day. As I'm sitting here, in comes: *don't forget about plants versus zombies later this is your son. Over and out.*

Perhaps due to my delicate emotional state, when I hear a siren outside and a dog howling back, calling and responding, two parts of a lost something, I become convinced that I need to go outside to find and pet the dog. But when I get out there, it's already gone. The only one standing there is Goblin. She was seeking the dog, too. Goblin's arms fall to her sides in defeat when she can't find her. I go and take a rest on her furry chest. She lays her hands on my hair so that I can find peace.

The thought of anything howling alone undoes Goblin and me. I get the dog's excitability though. Just how I feel when I look at the moon, my son dragging us to the grassy park down the block whenever there's a full one, so we can sit under those red-berried trees, howl at the full moon, and feel something madly distant calling to us in a way that feels close-up.

During those early pandemic days, when I worked late, I would peek through those windows at the moon and the one tree I could see out there, whose branches resembled a goblin's crooked fingers, wondering what exact day in the future I would die, and if I'd be, like, all mature about it. I'd been inhaling spirits at cemeteries for years now. I was ready to wrap my mind around it.

43. What is a Lyric Essay?

After trying unsuccessfully to find the howling dog, I stand in the incredibly long on-campus coffee shop line yet again to get another huge coffee from a "barista" who never knows to give me the donut I want, and whom I don't love half as much as Hector. As I wait, I answer emailed interview questions about the recent book of lyric essays I wrote. The first question is, *what is a lyric essay?* Good question. I email the interviewer that I think I wrote "fucking" instead of "funky" because autocorrect is out to get me. I wonder what Hector is doing and Google new jokes to tell him.

I get tired of the interview questions and try to work on a book list due later today, which is really a thinly veiled advertisement for my new book. There comes a surreal moment in the book promotion process where the introverted writer splits off from the person answering the interviewers and posting "exciting news" so that when they're like, *who's that insufferable person?* you can honestly be like, *never seen her before in my life.* I wake from literary self-promotion like a hangover: blurry, queasy, piecing together how I've made a fool of myself. Self-promotion is gross, but it does help me to remember its ancient roots, or how in 440 B.C.E. Herodotus sold *The Histories* to people at the Olympics, or how Whitman anonymously wrote shiny reviews of his own book, *Leaves of Grass* (now that is gross).

Yet, though self-promotion is unpleasant, don't go to the other extreme either and inadvertently shoot yourself in the foot when it comes to your work, as I often do. What not to do (all of which I have done) at book release events, for instance: don't discourage people from buying your book because it's too bizarre, or repeatedly make awkward jokes about how your dog actually wrote it, or about how mostly it's this dog that buys your books. Especially when you don't have a dog.

When I finally get to the front of the coffee line, I order and attempt to tell the barista a coffee joke. I do this because I misunderstand her false intimacy for the sake of tips for real intimacy and mistake her momentarily for Hector because she's giving me coffee. I sort of see it happening in slow motion that I'm telling a joke, and that it's not being well-received, but can't seem to stop myself. It's happening at the sluggish pace, in the same quasi-surreal sequence as when you realize, almost dreamily, that you're falling down a flight of stairs. What has gotten into me? Something is shifting. I've been doing things like this lately. Things that will please nobody. But will please me. My mom calls it *feeling my oats.*

What do you call a cow who's just given birth? De-calf-inated, I say to the Barista as she hands me my iced coffee. She looks, as I interpret it, horrified. I worry for a moment that I've turned her to stone, but then she asks if I want a straw, and I start to make a beeline for the cafeteria before I get the urge to tell another joke. I miss Hector terribly. But then the barista surprises me by calling out behind me, *wait, do you want milk?* I'm stunned that she would ever talk to me again after that terrible joke. Then she double-surprises me by adding, *the cow could use it to feed her calves!* with a goofy smile, and now I'm planning my double-wedding to Hector and the barista. I don't know what else to do, so I scrawl *thank you!* on a napkin with the coffee shop logo on it and run away. But when I turn back for a second before slinking into the cafeteria, she's waving excitedly, holding up the napkin. How had I so misread her?

I eat something resembling a sandwich from the cafeteria while trying to write a blog post on writing blog posts because I am very meta. Spill sandwich sauce on school computer. Rectify. Cackle. Attempt to write about this moment. Wonder if it's really living if you try to convert all the living into writing. Write that down. Get a text from my son that says, *the beef jerky wasn't delicious like you said it was! Over and out.* I never should have taught him walkie-talkie lingo.

44. A Descending Helix

I go to the college library to research recent books that have used hybrid forms to explore trauma. Think of what seems to be the beginning of some sort of manifesto, feel inspired until my phone rings, angering the librarian. Apologize. Feel like I apologize too much, which I know comes from my people-pleasing problem. Remember, as I do at least once a week, the two works I read whenever I feel a bout of people-pleasing coming on: Melissa Febos's essay on whether you want to be remembered for your writing or for your prompt email responses, and Carley Moore's essay on how, no, she doesn't have to get a coffee with you.

Right now, it's pretty clear to me that I will be remembered for my prompt email responses and not my actual writing, and this troubles me. Me: Nodding vigorously while reading seminal feminist essays on setting creative boundaries. Also me: then, instead of writing my new manifesto, proceeding to resurrect the lost art of letter writing by sitting there in that library and promptly replying to each email as though it were a child in need of an organ. But they lost athletics today. But also I can always find a reason why someone else's needs are more important.

Carley Moore's essay takes the form of a "descending helix," or the kind that, after Phillip Lopate, *follows a helically descending path, working through preliminary supposition to reach a more difficult core of honesty.*

Moore's essay is about literary structure, but also structures of violence, abuse, trauma, and people-pleasing, and how they are all more related than we might think. For instance, Moore points out how many victims blame themselves while their abusers feel just fine and dandy about how things went down. Like, my mind adds, even the worst kinds of abusers, men who keep girls in basements kind of abusers.

My horror every time I open a newspaper is that I will find another disturbing basement tale. What's scary isn't so much the mad woman in the attic but the little girl in the basement. I can tell you she will need Goblin down there, that Goblin will save her. Yes. That she will spend the rest of her life imagining Goblin to get through even a normal subway ride. That she will never go down the helically descending path to a basement ever again. No.

It reminds me of Ursula Le Guin's story of the suffering child in the basement that must be there for the village to be joyous. This tale always horrifies my students because it's really about how we will do anything to certain people so that we can sleep comfortably at night. This is Ta-Nehisi Coates' point about how *the dream* is built on the suffering of so many. This was Cathy Park Hong's point about minor feelings, or the erasure of any feelings that throw a question mark around the American dream, such as the feelings of the crying child in the basement in Le Guin's work.

How I wanted to storm down to that basement and rescue that child, who was also me. When I teach the story in class later that afternoon, through a show of hands, we will separate the room into those who would opt to rescue the child and those who wouldn't. Some will vote no because they don't know what would happen to the rest of the people, to their own children. Yes, and maybe it's not the best or most rational plan, but how can you leave that child suffering down there? The story is called "The Ones Who Walk Away from Omelas," Omelas being the name of the supposed utopia which is of course a dystopia. Le Guin catalogues the various ways the townspeople react to the existence of this imprisoned child. The last possibility she outlines is to walk away from this place altogether.

The first time I read the story, I was mesmerized by the image of the people who didn't just submit to this impossible scenario: either let the child suffer and have a good life or save the child and risk destroying everyone else. Instead, the ones who walk away choose option C: a hag brilliance, a march into the unknown. A revolt. Goblin mode. Where they are walking exists beyond what even Le Guin, with all her literary wizardry, can possibly describe. This place may not even be in the world, she tells us. What these people walk towards may be impossibility itself, but it also may be the chance to remake everything, to create a new world—and certainly one without a child crying in a basement. They walk beyond where the walking is meant to end. But they still don't save the child, and therefore I still can't sleep at night.

Carley Moore makes the connections between the coffee she doesn't have to get with you and trauma by pointing out how many of Weinstein's attacks began with requests for meetings that these women were just so used to saying yes to. Put it this way: I get 500 coffees a week; or put it this way: how many times a day do you ask yourself, *am I allowed to say no to this*? Way too often probably. I know I do.

As a card-carrying people pleaser and survivor, I feel seen by the connections Moore makes in her essay. I've spent the past years learning how not to please people. How to please myself. It's a work in progress. It takes forever to even hear the squeaky little voice of what I want after all these years. Part of what Moore unearths is how people-pleasing is linked to bodily danger, and people don't talk about it nearly enough. I will tell my daughter, though. I will do anything I can to keep her out of basements.

I'm growing older and needing to assert myself and not be so pleasing, and just take the risk that I might end up all alone in the end. I'm learning to write with that same honesty and realize that I might end without any readers in the end. This kind of writing is not for everyone after all. It's a conflagration, and frequently fragmented so it can cut you if you cross it in the night. It's also shame-inducing to write about trauma. Notice how I waited until this late in the book to talk more about this topic. I figured most people won't have read this far anyway, as you did, and this way it can just be our secret.

Moore wants you to know her essay structure is intentional, rigorous, carefully thought out, not a ditzy girl stumbling upon something in the bookish woods. Like how I graphed this book like I knew something about math, even though it feels like something I wrote drunk on the late train home last night. Moore orchestrates the structure to reveal societal structures that require our deeper consideration. As she tells us, after years of essay writing, she has learned that if she's obsessed with something tiny, it's probably connected to something larger that requires exploration. Let's bookmark that.

Through my endless reading on trauma, I find that Roxanne Gay embraces the term victim while Melissa Febos writes: *I have often wished for a different word, one that implies profound, often inhibitive, change, but precludes the wound and victimization.* This word becomes, *event.* She wants it to convey, *consequences rather than wounds.* Gay also calls for a rewriting of rape that conveys the brutality of it so people can't ignore the real lived bodily horror of it. Gay, as Chanel Miller does in her viral letter, and as the movie *Promising Young Woman* does in its own oddball way, reminds us to think of the promising young woman "victim" whose life is ruined rather than all these supposedly "promising" young men whose lives are "ruined" because they raped someone.

How people picture a "victim" doesn't resonate with me. It has nothing to do with me, in fact. How to explain that even people who have been torn apart and had to put themselves back together again can, I don't know, still chuckle and enjoy a good bacon, egg and cheese on a roll?

Plus, as Hannah Gadsby says, there's nothing stronger than a woman who has put herself back together. That she can still have particularities and not resemble a silent girl killed off to shape a dusty old Edgar Allan Poe rip-off story? That she could still have a sense of humor? That maybe that's at least partly what got her through? Telling goblin jokes in the basement.

Unlike stand-up comedy, so often written creative nonfiction forms that make serious points are humorless. I don't mean that trauma narratives should be cracking jokes all the time, but to be totally humorless can create limitations of reach, as in the case where I believe it's partially Chanel Miller's thoughtful deployment of humor that helped her letter about sexual assault and its legal treatment go viral. It told people: look, the "victim" is still human and can joke around while also nailing rape culture. How about that? Humor humanized Chanel so people had to care. Rather than the Jane Doe in the ditch that opens every TV series, she's multidimensional and alive; she lived to tell her story. She even made you laugh.

Carley Moore writes, *There's a complex mixture of fear, shame, desire, love and anger that so many smart women I know and love are carrying around right now. Are we fires that won't stop burning? Maybe there's no other way to live right now, but as inflamed, burning, every last one of us a phoenix.* Personally, I want nothing to do with the word victim. Please only ever call me a phoenix.

45. Dream House as Stoner Comedy

In her book, *In the Dream House,* Carmen Maria Machado explores abuse, and the creativity that can help to combat and process it, via different genres and rhetorical devices. There are chapters such as *Dream House as Inciting Incident* and *Dream House as Romance Novel.* Mind you, though this book covers traumatic territory, it's also a blast to read. Fun though it might be, it's built on weighty ideas, and this gives it a paradoxical flare as we zoom through *Dream House as Stoner Comedy,* but all against the backdrop of deeper narrative and cultural theories. After writing the book, Machado gave interviewers all sorts of different reasons for the fragmentary structure but, she said, eventually it came down to this—*You can't bring yourself to say what you really think: I broke the stories down because I was breaking down and didn't know what else to do.* To tell the story of being disassembled often requires new textual approaches that may even appear to disassemble themselves. But what Machado gets, what Moore, and Gay, and Febos get, is that to break down text isn't to break it; you take the fragments and you monster them together. Ideally, at the end of the day, you might find yourself with quite the written assemblage.

Back in the world of the college library, still trying to put myself back together after the flasher incident, I attempt to make a feminist joke to the librarian about how women apologize too much. It doesn't land well. I apologize again.

Here's the joke I don't tell the librarian: *A guy walks into a library. He strolls up to the counter and looks at the librarian dead in the eyes and screams 'I'll have a milkshake, please.' The librarian shushes him and sternly says in a whisper, 'Sir, this is a library.' The man immediately apologizes and whispers, 'I'll have a milkshake, please.'*

The call that angers the librarian is from my mom, who needs me to walk her through turning her computer on by pressing the "on" button and then turning on her blender by also pressing the "on" button. I'm here to report that my parents still have a landline that they both get on to ask how to use all the technology in their lives, most of which doesn't really qualify as technology. E.G.: another question for today concerning a Dutch oven.

My mom has a greeting card on her fridge of a dog saying, *the internet is fascinating* and a cat standing behind it, disgusted, replying, *that's the toaster oven.* I think that about sums up my parents' relationship to technology. This also reflects something more noble: how they can laugh at themselves. I make a mental note to buy them tin can phones for the holidays. They can store them next to the turkey bell. They'll laugh about the phone gag for months, sitting by the Christmas tree they inexplicably keep decorated in their house seemingly year-round. They provide no shortage of comic fodder and I treasure them for it.

I finally leave campus, go out of my way for another huge coffee because I have a problem, but this time from Hector. I tell him I'm writing something in which he features prominently. See him light up. This time, I've come prepared and looked up another coffee joke for him on my way. I deliver it with too much excitement for what it really is: *what do you call a sad coffee?* He looks delighted that I'm finally telling him a coffee joke. *What?!* he asks. *A Depresso.* He laughs with his full body to such an extent that I'm worried he'll capsize his cart. I resist hugging him by pressing my arms tightly to my sides. But with the moment we just shared, I don't really need to hug him. It's obvious. *I'll bring another joke next time*, I say, heading back towards campus.

I get back to campus. Apply to the big creative writing fellowship I apply to every year and never get, even though I know it'll just go to Jonathan Franzen in the end. Decide to leave the "world of letters" and become a circus juggler. Decide to return to "the world of letters." Refresh Submittable. Pray to the gods of "the world of letters" for a place at the table. Lose an eyelash, blow it, and wish to write a "Big Important Book" one day. Lose another eyelash. Wish for a sloppy taco. Break down, go out and get the sloppy taco.

Nobody has nailed the problem with (bad) writing in the "world of letters," and in many "Big Important Books" better than Kingsley Amis in Lucky Jim: *It was a perfect title, in that it crystallized the article's... mindlessness, its funereal parade of yawn-enforcing facts, the pseudo-light it threw upon non-problems.*

I write a page that throws pseudo-light on non-problems, delete it, and then reward myself with food obviously. I consume the sloppy taco with vim and vigor. Speaking of the "world of letters," one problem with MFA programs that doesn't get discussed nearly enough is all the talk of "craft" but not of the reality of finishing that draft by rewarding yourself for each new page with a sloppy taco. I quickly clean the red taco sauce off my face because I must pick up the kids, and I don't need to see members of the PTA looking like a satisfied vampire.

46. Still Hear the Moon

I pick up my daughter (jumps into my arms), walk a block, pick up my son (pretends he doesn't know me until we're far from school then jumps into my arms). He trots along telling me the whole history of his philosophy on everything from the beginning of time, pausing only for a well-delivered poop joke, which he has not yet outgrown. But neither have I. I laugh loudest. He says, *poop jokes aren't my favorite jokes. But they're a solid number two.* I write it on my hand so I can tell Hector tomorrow morning.

Then, with no transition or warning, both kids simultaneously tantrum as if on cue because he wants to go to Albemarle Playground and she wants to go to Greenwood Playground, but we are going to no playground, but to the library instead, because I have a hundred books on the history of New York City to return. To the mom who sees that I'm on the brink of public weeping and gives me a Tupperware of freshly made samosas: you reignite my stubborn and often baseless belief that there is good in this world, and I wish you every lovely thing. To the stunned mom with the perfect kid who gives me dirty look during the double tantrum: never do this again because it's icky. Thank you. I'm sorry.

As we walk home, I make a not-funny joke about the samosas. My kids laugh, but in that way where they don't understand but they're hoping I'll give them a treat. I give them a treat.

My daughter points with glee to the day moon. My challenge is to still see the moon amid the penises, and the endless needs of everyone around me that I feel fated to care for on a daily basis, the students lined up to cry in my office, sirens, insurance paperwork, PTA mixers, the spinning rock we live on hurtling towards oblivion. Is that how it works? I make a mental note to check at the library today now that my kids are finally on their way after the nice lady gave them lollipops. Never underestimate the power of bribery.

I try to frequent book places as often as possible before they go extinct. But I'll keep going regardless, even to the empty buildings. If they raze my local bookshop and library, I will go to pay my respects to what has been, my Library of Alexandria. I don't need something to exist in order to visit it. I've always been this way. This is why I'll still be hanging out with my father long after he's gone. We'll have booming grave parties and whatnot. But, until the library does go extinct, taking both my jobs along with it, I'll continue to drag my kids here to pay tribute to the human written word before it's all entirely penned by robots. I quickly rush my kids out of there today, though, apologizing profusely, after they get their lollipops stuck in a book.

47. Lil Nas X

After getting home, we rotate through our usual agony, ecstasy and gyrating on the mini trampoline while listening to clean versions of Lil Nas X on Spotify. I made the peanut butter and jelly sandwiches cut to resemble triangular monsters before I left this morning lest my kids experience storms of low blood sugar that would leave us all covered in blown-out pieces of nearby houses. I tell myself to try to find the sublime in these sugary triangles I must make every day because that's where I must look, so let it be there. How's it going? I'll have to get back to you on that one.

I cook dinner while wearing my Susan Sontag apron and playing Tom Waits' *Rain Dogs* for my lost high school self from the subway this morning. I allow the kids to help me, which means they make a giant mess they don't clean up and nothing gets cooked until much later. She wants to make smiley faces on the soft tacos with the beans and who are we to say this isn't how they were meant to be prepared? He wants to make the salsa look like blood coming out of the smiling mouth of the soft taco. I fear this will upset her but she's into it and, as everything does, the tacos become zombie tacos before my very eyes. We have moved so far past not playing with our food by now.

After reading Laura Esquivel's *Like Water for Chocolate,* I like to pretend I can put my feelings as magic into the food I make because

I'm still a child mentally. As I cut up the avocado and sear the peppers, I envision imbuing it all with a life of safety and passion for my kids in which they can bypass all the hurt, but as I look at the tacos with bleeding mouths, I see this is not possible, so I make due with attempting to eat dinner while the kids attempt to break the house. After dinner, instead of cleaning up right away, I chase them around with a sock puppet we call "Moppet." Hilarity ensues. You had to be there.

My son does that thing he does where he's suddenly thoughtful, says I look tired, and offers to do the dishes. My daughter goes to help him since she means well but mostly because she copies everything he does. I sit on the couch and stare at this phenomenon, a smile plastered on my face, in a state of shock. I'm afraid if I move, I'll disturb the dream. There are various plates and bowls broken but they have good intentions, and my daughter will probably use the shattered pieces in an art project that she involves my son in anyway.

And so everything goes mostly okay until that time of day when we all always melt down—when she cries heavily over the lurking perception that someone somewhere moved something in her labyrinthine "art area," which takes up most of my desk and now also the apartment floor; and as a result he gets angry and it all sends me to the closet to hide out while eating contraband snack food I smuggled in there.

From inside the closet, as the kids pound on the door and I tell them I'll be right out, I call my mom to ask her why life is so hard sometimes. She says that *without the bitter the sweet would be undetectable* and I find her to be in this moment very wise. It must be that British sense of humor. I ask how the turkeys are and she tells me they're currently taking a mud bath in front of her porch window and she's going to leave extra birdseed for them tonight. Without the children's meltdowns, the turkeys would be undetectable.

48. Fairy Godmother Voice

After I emerge from the closet, I ask ten times—in my fake-sweet fairy godmother voice that signals to all that I'm about to lose it—for them to stop bouncing off the walls before bed. They want to see how many grapes they can throw into each other's mouths before the Bad Bunny song ends, and I am trying to explain that this is simply not safe. As I'm starting to explicate choking hazards, he picks her up and asks if she wants to be used as a boomerang, and this is when I lose it. I've waded through the game playing in my bed since five, the sorrow of the athlete, the crying students, the crying children, my own crying, the bad jokes, the howling dog, the flasher, and now I'm done.

I've had it, so I pick up the huge yoga bouncy ball and bounce it against the wall like a child having a tantrum. There's stunned silence in the child peanut gallery, and I'm afraid they'll be scarred for life because God forbid they should see my humanity, see that I'm just them pretending to be something larger.

Through mental acrobatics and arcane tricks, I avoid losing my temper with them all that often, so they're not used to it. This can lead me to feel extra pissed and valid when I do lose it, as though I've earned the privilege of acting like a baby, though I have not. I stare at them, they stare at me, and then, luckily, we all crack up, doing impressions of me as an absurd baby.

It's yet another way that we've all chosen to laugh instead of cry, or what Nietzsche describes as an instance of *laughing over ourselves*, which he recommends since *nothing does us as much good as a fool's cap: we need it in relation to ourselves—we need all exuberant, floating, dancing, mocking, childish, and blissful art.*

The Nietzsche quote makes me return with fresh eyes to the way my daughter has transformed my working space into our shared childish and blissful art area. I see now that being creative with her (in the kid-like way I'd left behind in childhood before becoming a mother) is yet another way I've survived the pandemic and, well, everything. She has created what she calls her art studio that we're not supposed to touch. She adds to it like a nest or brain-in-progress. She has built up this environment, layering toy upon sketchpad upon glitter glue until it becomes its own strange brand of breathing being. I wait for it to speak to me each morning, feeling oddly sad when it doesn't.

It's geological, with layers like the makeup of the earth, except formed from paint-splattered coloring books, glow-in-the-dark slime, rainbow pipe cleaners, googly eyes, and Elmer's glue that has all run together to form a glitter-horror mass that makes up her creative life, but also hauntingly resembles my own. And there it is: my daughter has created a physical manifestation of my inner writing place, and I'm trying to speak to it. This is an example of what people mean when they say they feel super connected to their kids even as they drive them crazy.

After the whole bouncy ball thing, my daughter retreats to her art area. She has stacked up the *Dog Man* books that show you how to draw the characters. Her tongue pokes out of the side of her mouth and she squints, shoving her hair out of her face repeatedly, as she draws. I try to archive this sight somewhere I'll never lose it, where I can check on it from time to time. I feel bad about earlier, so I show her how to add speech bubbles. Above all, I want my daughter's characters (and my daughter) to have a voice.

49. Yes, Yes, Crayons

I understand my daughter's art mess because I make so much writing mess of my own. Once I have a first draft, I stare at something, let my mind grow blurry until I fasten on the pattern, and then I braid these fragments together (just as my daughter tried to braid scallions, or as she braids the pipe cleaners in her art swamp, my outlandish girl) with attention to these gleaned patterns, then graphing them to see where to position each sentence to make an absurd sort of sense, the kind you understand only in the middle of the night when your ceiling fan becomes a propeller to another galaxy and you are its queen.

Many writers spend their whole careers chasing that enchanted writing tip that will make their writing extraordinary. I read up on writers' habits and craft advice obsessively. Kurt Vonnegut insists that you avoid wasting the readers' time: every sentence should advance plot or character, or it shouldn't be there. He says to give each character a distinct need, even for something as simple as, say, a sandwich. Then, make your readers like at least one character so much they desperately want this character to get that sandwich. But he also says to be mean to your nice characters to remind your reader how resilient they are.

Vonnegut proposes composing with a single person in mind: *don't open the window and try to please the whole world or you'll catch pneumonia.* He's also against keeping too much information to yourself.

Instead, he says, give the reader so much knowledge of the book they could write the ending themselves, in the highly unlikely but entirely Vonnegutian scenario that cockroaches should eat it. Which is possible in Brooklyn.

Mark Twain suggests using *damn* instead of *very*, and letting your editor remove every instance as a public service. Elmore Leonard says to throw out the part readers usually skip, and William Faulkner and Stephen King call for the murder of your darlings: cutting those precious parts you love but others won't. In the interest of your writing career, Richard Ford suggests trimming the fat in a different way entirely, by not having children. Too late for that one over here, Richard Ford.

After you *kill your darlings*, I tell students to put them in a liminal place where they might live again, a huge file where you keep all your rejected dears. I call it my Graveyard File, and that's where I've been hanging out just now, trying to see if there's anything worth dragging out, while my daughter makes what appears to be her first graphic novel.

I try to get into a creative state, but my daughter runs over to show me her comic book, and how the main character, named Mommy, fights all the evil villains and ultimately turns into… But I never get to see what she turns into because my son runs in to tell us the neighbor's dog is back, and he's getting the peanut butter. *Get those faces ready,* I tell them, clomping along behind them to get this party started. By the time I come back to the computer, I've lost my writing concentration and I'm coated from head to toe in crunchy peanut butter.

Writers' rituals are central to the way they work and are often treated as acts of spirituality or even seance. Haruki Murakami refers to his routine as *a form of mesmerism* and gets many of his best ideas while running. Stephen King believes the exactitude of his morning schedule lets his mind know, in no uncertain terms, that it will be dreaming soon.

Each writer swears by a certain method to do the creative trick. Gustave Flaubert stuck to a schedule so firm his biographer, Frederick

Brown, described it as *unvaried as the notes of the cuckoo*. It also sounds quite exhausting. After having a light breakfast and applying his anti-balding ointment, Flaubert would work from one p.m. to one a.m. Biographer Judith Thurman credits Colette's robust health and writing life in her late fifties to gymnastic sex and hanging out with younger people.

James Thurber would compose all the time in his head, to the extent that his wife often had to say, *Dammit, Thurber, stop writing*, as my son says to me (minus the *dammit*). Thurber did this partly out of passion but partly due to bad eyesight. When he did physically write, he did so with black crayon on yellow paper, but he really got cooking when he could dictate to a secretary.

Franz Kafka had to fit work in between shifts at the Workers' Accident Insurance Institute, so he wrote from eleven p.m. to the early morning hours, between one and three a.m. and sometimes even six a.m. His literary executor Max Brod thought Kafka's parents should have provided for him financially so he could *create those works that God, using Franz's brain, wishes the world to have*, but Kafka seemed to do just fine on his own.

Clearly, I mostly get interrupted from any sort of creative trance by the kids. I write this as I wipe peanut butter from my computer screen and lick my fingers. With three children, Alice Munro could only write while the kids napped or while something was baking. Also a mother, Toni Morrison started her work before 5 a.m. because that's when at least one of the kids would call for mama. But her choice of early morning goes deeper. For her, being there to greet the light, cup of coffee in hand, is her way of entering what she calls, *a space I can only call nonsecular*.

I enjoy this idea of the creative space as a nonsecular one. But the antic nature of my kids has resulted in my total lack of replicable writing ritual. I write on my phone's notes section in the movie theater during the previews, on the toilet, in closets, on napkins, on my kids' drawing paper, on the donut floats at the lake by my parents' house, in moving cars, stalled subways, even on the slower Deno's Wonder Wheel Amusement Park rides at Coney Island, on my own skin, and, like Thurber, always in my mind.

I used to feel sad about all I didn't write, about all the books I didn't finish, all the things I didn't do. But now I see that everything I read—full books and fragments, student papers, lit submissions, parking signs, status updates, receipts, recipes, notes on bar napkins— and even everything I didn't write lives inside me as this enormous, unruly, best book of all time. We are all these strange archives.

The piece of Morrison's routine that really resonates is finding that space that I can only describe as mystical. Because I can never find the same place or time to write, or any reliable peace, I have had to learn to click my mind into that space, even as my children ransack the house. The only way I can put it is to say that there's normal brain and then there's writing brain, and I must teleport there no matter what's going on around me. One way that I cheat or augment this teleportation process is by thinking of the writers I worship. I have them up over my writing desk, as my computer screensaver, and always in my mind's eye. Thinking of them, of the audacious work they have achieved, helps me travel to my nonsecular place, even if my unruly progeny are hurling plates of spaghetti and meatballs at my head as I do so. Or in this case, even if I am trying to make love to these zombie taco leftovers.

Maybe it's genetic. When my daughter works in her "studio," she stares into space then takes crayon to paper like she's possessed. And my son told me the other night that he does the same thing while playing chess: he stares at the wall until his eyes get blurry to turn his daydreaming switch on. Since I was a kid, I've been doing a similar thing, where I stare until I start to see these floating dots that I imagine are my inner solar system projected outward.

Kurt Vonnegut outlined *Slaughterhouse Five* on wallpaper with his daughter's crayons. When my daughter asks me one night what I mean by creativity I say, *like when you sit here and scribble so hard with your crayons they almost break and it feels magic and maybe a little freaky*, and she agrees, *yes, yes, crayons*. What really goes on inside children, particularly before they have language, but also after? Do any of us truly have the words we need? And do we really have the answers when kids ask the tough ontological questions, like my daughter does this evening: *You can't hold the whole world in your hands, though, right? That's just a song?*

I don't have time to ponder the potentiality of carting around the entire world, or to write the next great American novel right now. I must get everyone into bed because we're catching a red eye tomorrow morning to spend Christmas in Puerto Rico with my parents. And, as all parents know, there's nothing more miserable than flying with two hyperactive kids by yourself. So, if you never hear from me again, it's because some guy on the plane brained me after my kid accidentally kicked the back of his seat. There will be a viral video of it seconds after it happens and you can watch me finally unravel. Because, not gonna lie, that's the sociopolitical climate we live in right now. A murderous one.

50. Bioluminescence

My father used to work in Puerto Rico, so we return every Christmas. I don't die on the plane at the meaty hands of an angry man, so that's something. We fly in early on Christmas morning, celebrate with my parents and some family friends, and then at night I take my daughter to see the bioluminescent bay.

Bioluminescence is the ocean version of fireflies, or when marine creatures illuminate the ocean through chemical reactions as they seek to protect themselves and communicate. So, what we are seeking is the defensive light language of sea animals, a visually pleasing form of survival, or that's what I tell myself as I belt out *I Like to Move it* from *Madagascar* one hundred and fifty times so we can drive with minimal conflict to Fajardo.

This water will be a far cry from the East River I usually walk along to ogle the simultaneous visions of the Brooklyn and Manhattan Bridges. If you stand there, by the fence that separates you from the river, there are places where, when windy enough, the water splashes up into your face a little. I walked there after reading Maggie Nelson's *Bluets* and realizing that maybe I could write prose one day if that was prose. It was a bit of an aha moment for me. Soon after my big realization, my daughter threw the book over the fence and into the East River.

But have I ever truly learned to write prose? Or is everything I write still poetry? And does it really even matter? What are the qualities, formal innovations, and associative leaps that a poet brings to prose? What separates, distinguishes, or defines the poet's novel or nonfiction (outside of it being written by a writer who is known as a poet)—and should it even be pushed into the rigid categories inherent in any act of definition? I can never seem to make my language work in the exact way prose writers typically do. Even as I learn new techniques of pacing and plotting, there always sticks to my words something of the land of poetry. Just as, ever since I had my kids, I feel I trail my childs' world into my daily work life where I playact as an adult.

I often find my prose making certain poetic associative leaps that ask the reader to find some of the meaning inside themselves. I can just barely fit the body of my words inside the prose door. Which is all to say that maybe calling it a "poet's novel," for instance, is too limiting. Maybe when poets write novels, they are creating something entirely new, which reflects a monstrous coming together, as when woman and fish make a mermaid. At the very least, this creature should really have its own fun name,—*Noem*? *Povel*? *Novem*? Suggestions welcome. My daughter says I should call the books I write *poopems* and it's not the worst idea. I explain to my son that my ideal form for this book mixes the essay, novel, and poetry forms. He suggests calling it a *poessayvel* and I'm smitten with this moniker.

Like many other writers and city dwellers, Whitman too was astounded by the Brooklyn Bridge. While it was being built, he wrote: *To the right the East river—the mast-hemm'd shores—the grand obelisk-like towers of the bridge, one on either side, in haze, yet plainly defin'd, giant brothers twain, throwing free graceful interlinking loops high across the tumbled tumultuous current below.*

Hart Crane's book-length love letter to the Brooklyn Bridge also mentions good old Whitman. *Walt, tell me, Walt Whitman, if infinity / Be still the same as when you walked the beach / Near Paumanok—your lone*

patrol; and, yes, Walt, Afoot again, and onward without halt,—Not soon,
nor suddenly,—never to let go My hand in yours, Walt Whitman—so—

The Brooklyn Bridge, its towers set to be on par with the highest
New York buildings, was completed in 1883 after a complex and
conflicted building process in which some died, including its first
engineer, John Augustus Roebling. His son Washington took up his
work after, another Telemachus son following the clever workings of
a lost Odysseus father. Those who labored at the bottom of the East
River got the Bends. Washington also got it and finished his work on
the Bridge from his Brooklyn Heights apartment, from which he could
see the ambitious structure he was constructing. Like how when my
phone glows at night, I wonder if it's my writing trying to reach me.

Crane would actually go on to live in the same building as bridge-
builder Roebling, 110 Columbia Heights, with its striking bridge
panorama. Crane raved to his mother about *the finest view in all*
America. Just imagine looking out your window directly on the East River
with nothing intervening between your view of the Statue of Liberty, way
down the harbor, and the marvelous beauty of Brooklyn Bridge close above
you and on your right! I hear Crane on this one. Like the subway, the
Brooklyn Bridge is a conceptual fulcrum for me. It connects different
parts of my city, and I often picture this structure when making the
outlandish mental connections necessary to write. I Brooklyn Bridge
the eagle idea to the human notion to the lion concept to make my
written Sphinx. Who's to solve its riddle? Please let it be you.

The bioluminescent bay will also be strikingly different from the
swimming experience my kids usually have—riding the F train to
the southern tip of Brooklyn, Coney Island, to bathe in the sea with
probably a bunch of corpses floating around. This island haunts one of
my favorite poetry collections: Lawrence Ferlinghetti's *A Coney Island*
of the Mind, in which he explores the complexity of his own inner isle
by way of Brooklyn. He writes, *I once started out / to walk around the*
world / but ended up in Brooklyn, / that Bridge was too much for me.

From 1885 through 1896, the hotel-cum-brothel, the Coney Island Elephant, was the first thing New York newcomers would see as they sailed in. What would they find when they landed? An encyclopedic array of vice: prostitution, gambling, "freak shows," and in modern times, the worst crime of all–buying those over-priced piña coladas on the boardwalk. Originally called Narrioch, or land without shadows, by its Native population, and later Conyne Eylandt by Dutch Coneyites, the Island was once the site of a booming resort and amusement park. It reached its peak in the mid-twentieth century and started to decline after World War II, becoming by the twenty-first century the endearing mess I've come to love.

In *A Coney Island of the Mind*, Ferlinghetti moves his reader through a geography of mental and written space. Even his title implies the creation through words of a socially important actual location (Coney Island) transported to the realms of the mind, or a psycho-spatial place that Ferlinghetti creates though his poetry. Coney Island performs a similar service. A thrilling combination of life forms, Coney Island is one of the few places in New York where you'll see a yuppie and a Hells Angel crunched together on the Cyclone, raising their hands together as they go over the first drop.

The first time my son rode the Cyclone, he'd just read *The Lightning Thief*, the first book in Rick Riordan's *Percy Jackson and the Olympians* series. It could have been that he was nervous but, for whatever reason, throughout the entire ride, even during the steepest part of the descent, he didn't stop telling me about the origins and play-by-play plot of the book. He'd spent the subway ride there reading up on Rick Riordan's motivations for writing the books on Wikipedia.

My son from New York City with ADHD who's obsessed with Greek myths was thrilled to find, in *The Lightning Thief*, this myth-obsessed, New York native with ADHD, Percy Jackson. What I discovered on the Cyclone was that in particular my son was—I don't know how else to put it—simply gobsmacked that Riordan had invented these tales to soothe his son, who also had ADHD and had learned about the Greek myths in school, at bedtime. When the mythological well ran dry, his son suggested he invent new myths, or rather the old ones but with crucial twists, leading to the story of Percy trawling America in search of Zeus's lightning bolt.

Percy suspects Hades of possessing said lightning bolt, so he must descend into the underworld to retrieve it. Where exactly is the land of the dead in Riordan's telling of the myth? In Los Angeles. My son didn't get why this was funny to me and it would have taken too long to explain about celebrity culture, so instead I said, *hands up, we're about to drop.*

My son looked down into the expanse he was speeding towards and blanched. But instead of being rendered silent by his apparent terror, he just started talking even faster. He told me about Percy descending into the under-realm, as he probably felt he was doing right then, careening towards death, or rather post-existence. Except that I was squeezing his raised hand so hard he knew I wouldn't let that happen and that, if it did, I'd become hybrid like Percy, part mortal, part immortal—part human, part Fury, that ancient Greek deity of vengeance.

After we survived that first drop and kept lurching forward, my son said, *you know the best part? The author made ADHD why Percy is so good at doing superhero stuff, because he like has good reflexes and everything and how his mind works differently like being able to read ancient Greek but not really so much English.*

51. Swamp Aliens

Not only is the bioluminescent bay not Coney Island, but the initial safety talk we receive doesn't make the trip seem like the spiffy little jaunt we had initially expected either. I thought it would be fine even though I hadn't kayaked in years, even though I would essentially be kayaking alone since my six-year-old daughter was more likely to fall overboard or be abducted by swamp aliens than helpfully paddle in front.

She was so excited, asking me for weeks ahead of time when exactly we were going to see the lights, singing on a loop *Under the Sea* from *The Little Mermaid* movie. She'd even said if she saw the lights before me, she'd shut her eyes tight until I could see them too, so we could definitely see them at the same time. I thanked her, my mind feeling around for what recent event convinced her of this plan. She's still young enough, her orbit tiny enough, that I know many of her touchstones. This will soon change. What I mean is, what made her think I'd be angry if she saw the bioluminescence before me, if we didn't have the experience simultaneously? Finally, I just broke down and asked her. *Oh,* she said, getting very serious, *you said to wait to eat until everybody was sitting.* That I did.

But when we get to the bioluminescent bay, I realize it may be a bit more ornate than I'd imagined, involving two hours of paddling through mangrove swamps, against the current, in the dark. The website listed the age as six and up, but I don't see any other kids here.

After cracking some jokes and telling us he loves Bad Bunny, which makes me trust him since my son also makes us laugh and loves Bad Bunny, our guide's trying to be funny when he says, *don't worry, nobody is going to die out here, or are they?* But it's not funny right now and makes me feel pretty sure somebody's going to die out here. I wonder if we'll eventually recover Zeus's thunder bolt here in the land of the dead.

The guide makes the comment in response to the many, admittedly over-the-top, safety concerns of one participant in particular, but it makes it sound as though a life is something you could misplace under a mangrove, although maybe it is. The guide's joke only succeeds in rotating my thoughts again towards impermanence, our only permanent thing.

But my mind was already on such things because earlier that morning I'd been hanging out with my dad, who was sick, and now one hundred and twenty pounds at six feet tall, but still, luckily, with a fully intact sense of dark humor. We'd been taking turns reading to each other from a book about philosophies of death because that's the sort of thing we do for fun in my family. *Quick, what sort of ghost would you be?* I'd asked him. *A stylish one,* he said like he'd been waiting for me to ask, crossing his withered but still stylish legs in their weather-inappropriate loafers that had seen better days.

My dad and I both tend to take an approach to tragedy somewhere between detective and court jester: we make dark jokes about the thing because it breaks our heart, but we also try to attain an encyclopedic understanding of it. Maybe it's magical thinking, like if we can just crack the case, maybe we can reverse the course. My father is even like this with his own cancer, and I have followed his lead. I will for sure write about whatever future disease it is that will do me in. Plus, he tells jokes about it. Maybe this is why I love Hector, who gives me coffee and makes me laugh even in the early morning: because he reminds me of Dad. My father earlier today, on Christmas morning no less: *Oh, here's one I haven't told you yet. A doctor says, 'The good news is it's all in your head. The bad news is it's brain cancer.'*

My father was reading to me about how Buddhists meditate on death to embrace life. He said scientists have theorized multiple possibilities of how the world will end, pinning on this ending ominous, but admittedly catchy, titles such as The Big Crunch and The Big Freeze, wherein the universe (I am demonstrating my lack of understanding of science here) expands or collapses, folding in on itself in a series of deaths and rebirths. I find the concept of meditating on death useful. Then there's also the peppy news from quantum physics: we never really die but get remixed!

52. A Tour Book for the Afterlife

They don't bother giving my daughter a paddle as we set off from Fajardo and I believe it's better that way. My brave girl enjoys it at first. The bats flying around—visible only when the moon shines on them through the mangroves—are initially novel. Briefly, it's a Disney ride to her. We shriek but all in good fun.

She voices the different things we pass, doing impressions of what the various plants and animals might sound like or say. She does the Mangroves, she does the bats, she even does other kayakers until I put a stop to it before anyone gets offended. The others on the trip find her funny and ask her what this or that piece of landscape might say, culminating in her doing an impression of the moon that none of us will soon forget. She growls, in the voice of an old man who has drunk too much whiskey and smoked too many cigars, *argh, I'm the moon, and I'm sick and tired of it.* This phrase *sick and tired* is something she has picked up from my mom, and it all comes full circle out there in the swamp. The moon does seem a little tired tonight, hiding behind a yellow haze. It also appears to be preternaturally huge, maybe because we're used to so many things standing between it and us—buildings, pollution, thoughts of ourselves.

As I paddle, she wants to tell me about a movie she recently saw about a family of superheroes called *The Incredibles.* This of course involves telling me every detail from every scene and doing all the voices even though we saw the movie together. She is her grandmother's grandchild, her brother's sister, her mother's child. The stories in our family are our Mangrove roots, which bodes well for my kids since they are perfect habitats for the growth of young organisms.

Now, a bat grazes my cheek as it zips by. I don't want to scare my daughter, so I tell her I'm screaming because *I'm so excited about the sparkly water we're going to see.* But she sees through it. She always does. There's something patently haunted about the whole watery voyage and I show everything on my face. It outs me every time.

My hair is wet with sweat, and my daughter says, *you look scary, Mommy, like Cruella de Vil.* Here's the Cruella impression from *101 Dalmatians* I don't do at this point for fear that my daughter would disembark from the craft: *Any way you want. Poison them, drown them, bash them on the head. Got any chloroform? I don't care how you kill the little beasts, just do it, and do it now!*

I come from generations of parents passing on a camp relationship to the occult to their kids during playtime. My father used to do this eerie, screeching voice that was Ghosty, the ghost he claimed lived in our apartment and talked only to me. Before you start retroactively dialing child services, it's important to understand that I wasn't scared of Ghosty but thrilled, which I suppose tells you a little something about the kind of kid I was. I'd tell Ghosty all about my day, and even confide in Ghosty when my parents were bothering me. Whatever the issue was always got better afterward because Ghosty…was my dad. Ghosty's voice was hilarious, squeaky, high-pitched, shrill, terrible really. An older guy doing the voice of a young ghost.

But if you think about it, it's still an odd thing for my dad to do, for me to love, and so forth, and it accurately characterizes my childhood with its creative-absurdist-haunted undertones. It also reminds me that my son's darkly bizarre sense of humor is generational, starting with my father, and perhaps earlier if I went on a heritage deep dive. I used to wonder if Ghosty knew Goblin.

But really wasn't Ghosty (and Goblin) just an early experience of writing, too? This is the strangeness of reconstructing the past as a writer. My dad wrote the Ghosty script and I essentially read it. When we write, we are bringing back to life the dead. We are the taboo, moving against nature, asking that time dance in a different order than it might have, sinning, engaging in the uncertain act of memory, a risky business indeed, coming back with something that is part that time and part this time. We are messing with the spaciotemporal order. When I write about the past, I cause my woman self and my girl self to hang out and this is not natural. They do a goblin dance together in a field of memory. Maybe all writing is a time machine. Goblin mode.

53. Tibetan Book of the Dead

But as we enter hour two of the search for bioluminescence, the mood shifts from haunting yet fun, filled with expectation, to a plain old bad trip. It starts pouring rain, my daughter starts crying and saying she wants to go home, asking why I did this to her (no guilty feelings after that one, no siree) while I feel the same way, my arms numb, callouses starting to form, but we're already too far out to go back.

I try to make her laugh by doing a Cruella de Vil impression. Don't worry, it wasn't the one I did for you earlier. It was this one: (picture me crossing my eyes and doing a Glenn Close voice) *From the very beginning, I realized I saw the world differently than everyone else. That didn't sit well with some people. But I wasn't for everyone. I guess they were all scared… that I'd be… a psycho.* She always laughs at that one but not tonight.

It's time to whip out my secret weapon, which always used to soothe her when she was inconsolable as a baby. I start singing the two songs with the same tunes I used to sing to her in succession, *Twinkle Twinkle Little Star* and *Baa Baa Black Sheep*, in a weak effort to provide cheer. It's also worth noting that there's a darker stanza to the song that I never sing my daughter. Perhaps you've heard it: *When the blazing sun is gone, / When he nothing shines upon, / Then you show your little light, / Twinkle, twinkle, all the night.*

But then, to remind me that people can be good, the rest of the kayak trip starts singing it to her together after I lose my voice. The man who had all the safety concerns covers us all in his deep baritone, and I feel guilty for teasing him a little in my mind earlier. I send good tidings to him and all his descendants as we all paddle along, singing. Deep in the mangroves now, my mind turns again to thoughts of the afterlife.

When I worry about death, I like to think of the Bardo, or the pitstop between death and rebirth. *The Tibetan Book of the Dead* is like a tour book for the afterlife, before you're reborn—where are the best restaurants to eat sort of thing. But in all seriousness, it's meant to be read to the dead and this is a powerful thing. I love a genre meant for the deceased.

My dad contains an unexpected mixture of qualities. He's an old southern guy who was a businessman type for years, an engineer originally, who then became a psychoanalyst specializing in dreams in his fifties. Well before he got sick, he went on a dream journey to Mexico and took peyote, probably while wearing his preppy clothes and neon socks my mother buys him. He'll often rock a medicine bag over a knit polo, close to his heart. He has been studying the problem of mortality for years. He specializes in liminal states, in conceptual borderlands: in dreams and death. And now he's become his own guinea pig. *So many people see a light that beckons to them in near death experiences*, he often tells me. What could it be? *I wonder what I'll see*, he says. I wonder what we all will.

54. Dick Johnson is Dead

You should see my dad's night table. He's read all this stuff, including *The Tibetan Book of the Dead*. Maybe it's genetic, but I also like to read about mystical approaches to death and life. Will this help either of us let go of each other when the time comes? I wonder. I heard Daniel Day Lewis broke down crying while playing Hamlet because he thought he saw the ghost of his father. The novel I recently wrote has tinges of *Hamlet*: a character who reminds me of my dad dies but visits the daughter character as a ghost. The character even tells cancer jokes.

Filmmaker Kirsten Johnson made a wacky but profound documentary called *Dick Johnson is Dead*, where she stages ridiculous ways her elderly father with dementia, whom she adores, could possibly die. Her dad was a psychiatrist, so he gets it. It's cinematic therapy, theater of the absurd because very real; it's Ghosty. She has him repeatedly playact dying in slapstick panoramas so that they can rehearse this unrehearseable future loss, meditate on death and impermanence, and find that darkly humorous tunnel in which they can laugh to keep from crying. Apparently, to sell him on the idea, she said, *Dad, what if we make a movie where we kill you over and over again until you really die?* And he laughed. I almost want to ask my own dad to do this, except I have some limits on how conceptual I can really be about his illness.

As I paddle the kayak, I work more in my head on this book you're now reading. It's what I'm doing pretty much all the time that I'm awake, a Coney Island of the Mind. My father claims I work on it while I sleep too via dreams but that's another story that I'm not qualified to tell.

I almost lose the paddle as I see that this book takes up the exploration of potential father loss yet again, and how all my books just chase my obsessions over pathways of genre and are essentially networked. What sort of a metaverse does that enact for you? I picture you traversing these ragtag neural networks, pieces of my brain that I've huffed and puffed until they dangle outside of me, and I pity you. Just as I'm about to apologize to you, though, I see Goblin shaking her head, and I double down. Not another unnecessary apology. Instead, I just want to thank you for being here, and rest my head on your chest so you can pet my hair. Is that okay with you?

But, hopefully, I don't have to even deal with losing my dad. Instead, I'll bust us out of this ecosphere and transport us to an alternate reality. There, when he says his final goodbye, I can just construct something and call him back, write him back to life. According to movie mythos, building can also be a way of calling dead parents home, as it was for Kevin Costner in *Field of Dreams*, who hears, *if you build it, he will come* in reference to the baseball diamond and his father respectively. When I was little, my mother told me that after she dies, I can just speak to the moon, and she'd hear me—and she wonders why I became a poet and basically haunted. I still think of her every time I see the darn shining thing. This seems appropriate since the moon has always been associated with the mysteries of women. And who could be more mysterious than my *sui generis* mother?

The guides on the bioluminescent bay tour tell us to stop paddling, seemingly in the middle of the ocean, to look for the illumination we've come to find. They add that it's not such a great night for it, and they will need to cover us in huge tarps so we can make out the light. *I don't want to see the stupid fairy lights anymore* roars my daughter who's done doing impressions for now. Her hair is snaking all around her face, which is rubied from sobbing. She says she's scared but, it must be said, that she also looks, frankly, pretty frightening herself. *It doesn't look like we are going to see the stupid fairy lights after all*, I croak, having lost my voice. It must be said that I also sound, frankly, pretty frightening. She's quiet after that. I reach out to draw her hair out of her eyes and she flinches. I get really close to her ear and force my throat to make a little walrus sound, and this actually does seem to help. She makes a little one back at me, nuzzles me, and it lets me know she's still in there.

As we pass the tarp to those next to us, preparing to duck under it, the Bad Bunny guide "jokes," *and here is where we kill you*, laughing, but it doesn't seem like laugh material at all. Not one bit. *That's not* nice *mister bunny,* my daughter scolds him, braver than her mom already. He looks cowed, quietly passing the tarp now, no more jokes about death, put in his place by a six-year-old who currently resembles Medusa.

Now it hits me—after COVID, climate change, and more sociopolitical chaos than I can quantify—that we might be about to die out here on the open ocean. I wish Goblin would come and save us. But it will have to be me. I have to woman up and not require my six-year-old daughter to do my battles for me.

When I look up, lo and behold, above the guide's head is Goblin. I'm angry that the guide said the death thing at all, and most of all in front of my daughter. I want to confront him about it. I can see that Goblin wants this too, as her eyes grow enormous, rivaling the moon, and are aimed right at him, telegraphing my lifetime of not standing up for myself against men at key moments. I can't bring myself to say anything. I've lost my voice literally but what could be more metaphorical at this point? But I vow that I will rise up against the next person who crosses me. Little do I know how soon next time will come. Goblin sinks behind the moon.

55. Bad Bunny

My dad carries around a quote from Shelley's "Ozymandias" on a yellowed paper scrap in his pocket: *My name is Ozymandias, King of Kings;/ Look on my Works, ye Mighty, and despair! / Nothing beside remains. Round the decay / Of that colossal Wreck, boundless and bare / The lone and level sands stretch far away.* He jokes that he's an elegiac form, already gone. *Dick Johnson is Dead.*

At least we can joke about death together. He's always been an escapist, though not literally—no Houdini hijinks in our living room—but his mind was often mentally elsewhere. He was a non-professional filmmaker, a home movie maker, who spent a large part of my childhood behind a video camera asking me about the world, channeling his idol, Fellini. I rose to the occasion, a performer, a comedian, a writer, weaving a fictional persona even that early. A ham. Class clown. Always all about alternate realities. For reasons of survival and invention.

There was just so much that nobody knew about me. And I still need to keep the details for myself. This holding on to a sort of secrecy, even as I'm baring everything is so native to me it's hard to let go. In writing, I have always thought of myself, confessionally speaking, on an intellectual level, as a very private stripper. Getting to know me is still a dicey scavenger hunt. Even my written confessions are misleading. As

Poe knew, there's no better place to hide a secret than in plain sight; or to throw out a smaller one, part distraction, part sacrifice, sometimes just a red herring entirely. I'm so used to being elliptical, I'm not sure I've ever fully let anyone but my kids in. But I want to. I think.

I peek out of the tarp, under which I'm seeing no luminescence, at the guide. It could be because I've now cast him this way, but he looks foreboding. No longer friendly and smiling, he resembles a different person, part of his face lit by the moon, the other in darkness.

If these men want to kill us out here among the mangroves, who will stop them? I try to remember how Percy vanquishes Hades and leaves the underworld. I wish I could ask my son the right way. He always has all the answers. What can they really gain from killing us, though? This thought comforts me as I try to stay rational. Unless they just enjoy killing tourists? I've seen that movie a thousand times and really don't need to see it again.

How could the nice man guide who loves Bad Bunny do such a thing? But also, I'd felt I had to be prepared for disaster since the start of COVID, since September eleventh, since childhood maybe. My youth had taught me the supremely worthy skill of survivorship, and I'm not about to just die out here on the ocean, especially not with my daughter, who's funnier than most people, calls the Botanical Gardens the Mechanical Gardens, and does an impression of Weird Al Yankovic because she's mine. She's doing it right now, in between bouts of crying under the tarp, to cheer us all up, herself most of all.

How will I save her? If the guide wants to kill us out here, what sort of resources do I have to protect her? I have no mermaid tail, only human legs, and bowed ones at that. But I will find a way. Mark my words. I hear that rumbling sound inside me that means I'm getting ready to persist. I will become Goblin if necessary.

56. Literary Odyssey

Clearly, I've been watching too many disaster movies lately, which are coming out endlessly because we're all living through a disaster movie. What's more, I had arrived in Puerto Rico to find my father just deteriorating in front of me. He'd needed a wheelchair to get through the airport. My mom feared it was his last year coming here.

Earlier on this day of the bioluminescent bay, I'd sat with him on the beach and hugged him too hard and talked incessantly. He often says he's the boxer from the Simon and Garfunkel song since he keeps coming back from the almost dead again and again, which makes him kind of like the gothic creatures we both love to read about. We have sped to the intensive care unit again and again, thinking it was the last time, but he bounces back. Because he is the boxer.

Our connection has always been so much about reading and writing. For example, here's an email he sent me this morning right after we arrived in Puerto Rico: *Just back from beach, walked to your special spot where waves clash together on the point between beaches and chanted, your dream, the Art Monster, then back to the pool where chanted to Reggaeton.* I'm not sure why it had to be Reggaeton, but these are the wacky thought patterns peculiar to my parents.

My dad gets how way too seriously I take my *literary odyssey* as he calls it. He sends me Virginia Woolf quotes when he can't sleep, noting with glee that she did much of her best work later in life—hope for both of us. An email he sent me: *Woolf wrote Dalloway, Lighthouse, and Waves in her forties. Your turn. Room of One's Own sets the challenge for you.* No pressure, though, right? Only a father with a loose connection to reality would believe his daughter could be the next Virginia Woolf. But, of course, I love him for it. Who else is going to think that? We all need our person who believes we are something greater than we are.

After he read my last book, which touched on the art monster idea, he sent me this three-a.m. missive: *The magical thing: you have become truly yourself, no longer recognizable as my little daughter, but a monster of your own making.* A goblin?

57. Weather Disasters

I wanted to tell my dad something to help him hold on. Knowing him as I do, I said he should chronicle his voyage towards death. A memoir about his brushes with the underworld and the changes/ experiences in consciousness, especially since people find these narratives fascinating, and he's credentialed to do this after a life of studying states of consciousness both personally and professionally. He seemed to like the idea, but does he have enough pep left to do it? I just know a writing project would make him hold on. We're alike in this way. If I'm ever in the hospital, please bring me writing implements.

I realize suggesting to my dad that he chronicle his way out might sound insensitive to most, but in our family it's just that writing has always been our language of love. And didn't I just write a whole novel where the dad dies of cancer but comes back as a ghost, so the daughter doesn't truly have to lose him? Wasn't that my love letter to my dad? And aren't I writing this book to grapple with many of the same issues? I'd been nervous to ask how he felt about that novel idea in which he dies off and comes back as a ghost so I could face my fear of losing him. *Dick Johnson is Dead.* But he'd found the idea invigorating, sensing that in these pages he could find eternal life. Nobody told him about my Amazon sales rankings.

I worry sometimes that I shouldn't chronicle any of his experiences for him because it's like stealing his story, but every time I ask him, he says he loves how he will live on in my tales. I still can't believe how he went for the idea of becoming a ghost in my book and talked to me about *Hamlet* for a full hour. I listened intently, able to see rising above our heads both of our goblins, the portal where our reality overlapped with our attempts to rewrite it, not quite a secular space, shall we say. Goblin mode.

Was I trying to get my dad to write a sibling book to this one? Or perhaps it's more precise to say a father book to my daughter book? Our two books—which would have a family relation of course— chronicling our pain over his eventual flickering? That's the thing: so much of our meaning has been located through writing. Not even what it's about or what it signifies, but the act itself. So maybe I should just dig up his old video camera and film him at his typewriter, keep that tape forever under my pillow, stop trying to make this book work, and call it a day.

There's nobody out here on the ocean to hear our little group if we scream. We have no phones; we have nothing but our calloused paddling hands. We also have no money or valuables I remind myself, in favor or why they're not about to kill us. The Bad Bunny guide tells us it's time to pack it in. We're not going to see the bioluminescence, and I relax. I don't care about missing out on the glow. I'm just happy to be alive.

We don't see the light, but they also don't kill us, so that's a plus. Instead of dying on the water, we kayak back, the whole group singing "Twinkle Twinkle" again to my crying child whose life I luckily don't have to save.

That night, after we don't see the light in the bioluminescent bay but also don't die, I walk on the beach, stand at the peninsula, and feel the world coming in. Later, we watch *Encanto* outside, the Coqui frogs deafening, both kids on my lap, and my father beside me, holding my hand so hard it starts to tingle. I feel overwhelmed by how enchanted it is that we are alive right now. Who even knows if we can fly back and what sort of world we will be flying back to: increased weather disasters, rising fascism, civil rights dystopias.

At the end of a dark year for the universe, in the middle of *Encanto*, I get an email from my son's fourth grade teacher about the class magazine he's starting (?!) and how I might need to help him scan things, and I feel a jolt of anticipation. Writing will save us all.

58. Goblin Mode

This morning, after we got in late the night before from Puerto Rico, and everyone's exhausted, there's a substitute teacher in my son's class. So, I receive the sort of call I used to receive at schools I loved less about how he did something along the lines of dancing during singing time or singing during dancing time or some other school-scale apocalypse.

I laugh a little under my breath. Apologize. Inform her I'm on my way but can't pick him up for at least an hour, which is the normal pick-up time. I'm informed she guesses he can stay, but only if he sings during singing time and dances during dancing time. Not likely. Feel frustrated with all education systems ever. Decide to start a revolution. Realize I need to pee and am already running late. Pee while writing a grocery list on my phone's notes app. Must not forget more eggs for son. Must not forget to pick up son. Must not forget sun. Autocorrect. Must not forget. Son. Hurry out to get the kids. The revolution will have to wait.

On the way there, I give too much money to the Mariachi band that makes me ugly-cry with joy on the G train. Work on a few pages of the new book I'm editing by a writer I admire greatly. Wonder if I'll ever be as good as the woman I'm editing. Receive another rejection of my new book. Write a simultaneously sunny and breezy reply thanking them for their time while not feeling at all sunny or breezy. Wonder if they can sense it through the computer. Wonder if I'm supposed to reply to a rejection. Probably not. How do I not know the answer to this by now?

As we pull into Fourth Avenue and Ninth, but going in the other direction this time, an email dings in from someone who read my last book and felt less alone. I choke on gratitude and write her too long of an email promising her my next-born. Remember to tell writers what their work means to you. Every time I've lost faith in this rejection-heavy madness, someone has sent me a note about my writing that put me back together again. I may never win x, y or z award but I've kept all the notes. They're everything. I store them in a little puddle of hope in my Google docs.

When I finally look up, I notice my car is still almost empty. This is not unusual or necessarily cause for alarm. There was a man who got on with me at Hoyt and sat across from me. It was a little odd since the whole car was available and he chose there but, again, not unusual or cause for concern.

I text my father to ask how his new cancer medication is treating him, and he writes back, *it's like waiting for Godot*. On Christmas Day, our family friend showed the kids how to make origami cranes. He told them in Japanese culture you bring cranes for people who are sick as a blessing. So my daughter asked if we should bring some for Bebop, which is what she calls my father because he used to sing her "Be-Bop-a-Lula" by Gene Vincent and His Blue Caps.

I've taken off my contacts at the college to give my eyes a rest, so it takes me a little bit to focus in on exactly what I'm looking at. After I put on my glasses, it seems there's some beige fabric in the pants region of the man sitting across from me. But no.

When I look closer, what I'm seeing is that he has partially taken out his penis and is just sitting there, looking to see what I'll do next.

The weirdest part is how calm he appears. Like this thing, which is a time machine transporting me back to trauma, brings him peace.

I sit in stunned silence for a beat. Like all the women before me. Silent. Voice lost. Stock-still. Part of it is I don't know what's safe to do. We are in between stops, on that longer stretch between Fifteenth Street Prospect Park and Fort Hamilton Parkway.

But then when I look even closer, I see that it's the flasher from the college. It's him. Sitting across from me with his dick out.

Did he follow me here, so he's also a stalker? Or is this just one more coincidence thrown at me by a world with a sick sense of humor? Either way, I'm not having it. I don't accept it. Not today. Not anymore. I have entered Goblin mode.

I have an urge to just slink away. But then it all coalesces. Men have always done this, and I've never known how to stop it.

I see Goblin above his head. She's radiating so brightly she hurts my eyes. And now her body's on fire. It's shuttering back and forth above him. Flames are starting to tear through the subway car, and I feel I must act before the few other passengers are consumed. Cinders are starting to descend from Goblin. I lick the ash from my lips and position myself to fight.

She roars, *it's time,* and finally I nod in agreement. Today is the day I take action. I've finally had it. Something in me snaps.

But really, I had begun the rebellion earlier that morning when, seeing the sprawl of breakfast dishes, I had left them in the sink. I realize that this may not seem like the peak of insurrection but let me just tell you that it was big for me in my own small way.

These years have been too much for all of us, my kids pushing pictures they'd drawn for the immigrant kids kept in cages in Brooklyn under my door at all hours of the day. Then wearing masks, waiting in their school during gun threat lockdowns, and dodging subway shootings, the city turning orange from Canadian wildfires, rising white supremacy, racism being declared a public health crisis in New York City in 2021, just all of it. I know that everyone always feels they are living at the end of the world, and I get that it won't end tomorrow, but there is some bad stuff going down. COVID, the war in Ukraine, so many civil rights issues, so much other tragedy. Since 2016, just one long horrific meeting that should have been an email.

Right after so many of our kids' schools were locked down because of the Brooklyn subway shooting, we read *The Velveteen Rabbit*. My daughter asked me what "real" is, and I really couldn't say anymore.

Here, now, in the world of this man on the subway with his partially visible dick, I imagine an alternate reality in which I'm finally the superhero my kids often incorrectly imagine me to be, with time traveling powers. I become convinced that if I can stand up to the man on the subway, I can save my child self, I can save all the girls, all the boys, all the people. It's grandiose plus it doesn't make sense, but it's where I'm at right now. I even imagine taking this time machine back to whoever it was that hurt him because that's how these things start, isn't it? Just endless loops of trauma. I wouldn't hug him now for anything, but I'd go back in time and hug his child self if it would prevent him from doing this to me and other women down the line.

I'm so upset by the actions of this man that I'm momentarily inhabiting a parallel universe of goblins and superheroes over here rather than dealing directly with the situation. I decide my superpower is feeling the trauma of others. Shared sensations of suffering run through me all at once until I'm all but electrocuted. At last, I shriek, unsure if I'm in fact screaming in the world of the subway car, where the guy, it should be noted, still leisurely has his dick out.

I catch my own reflection in the darkened subway window as we speed through this hellscape. I'm horrified to find that I resemble Munch's painting *The Scream,* my face skull-like, mouth gaping, the poster of strawberries behind me standing in for the blood-red sky Munch saw as he had the sensation of *an infinite scream passing through nature* that he later tried to paint.

Goblin closes in, now rainbowed in protective power, holds me for one shattering second, then steps back, asks, *are you ready?* But when

I look over at our subway window reflection, there's just me standing there, a huge Fresh Direct poster of strawberries behind me like it's just any other Friday.

Suddenly, before I know it, my mouth has opened, I find myself screaming again but this time at the flasher: *That's all? Why don't you take the whole thing out? You think I'm scared of you? Do it!* He sits in silence, paralyzed, as I've done so many times. I almost start to feel for him. Almost. But not quite. I have so many other people to feel for. People who don't take their dicks out on the subway. People stuck looking at them.

The other passengers stare at us, looking like they want to help but are also afraid of what he will do, and maybe even what I will do. My whole extended family except for me was born in the South. Manners are so ingrained in me. I've never talked to anyone like this in my life. It feels bloody wonderful.

Goblin's lips part in a motion of unrepentant pleasure. I can see the purple insides of her mouth as she laughs with glee. Goblin's shaking the whole subway car with her maniacal laughter. Or is that me? It's like a *Fight Club* situation up in this piece, and I've been Tyler Durden all along. Surprise, motherfucker!

The flasher man looks small now. I almost pity him. Almost. But not quite. I must resist mothering him since he looks now like he might cry. But for once I need to resist protecting even the person who is hurting me and protect myself instead. But I can't yell anymore at someone who is now crying. I just don't have it in me.

Where does Goblin come from? I long to go there, a space beyond any I've ever ventured, a place where I could bray along with the other cattle of the sun, or whatever sound it is that solar cows make. Perhaps James Joyce, H.D. and my father will be there too, and we can all do the dance of the goblins together.

Why do you do it? I finally ask this man across from me on the subway. I just need to know.

He says, *I don't feel good about things. I don't feel good.*

I'm enraged. *Do you think I feel good? No, but do you see me whipping my dick out?* I growl at him until he turns into a tiny buzzing fly. Okay, no, but you see my point.

I'm holding a notebook. The train is pulling into Fort Hamilton. I drop the notebook in his lap, saying, *well, don't whip your dick out again on somebody. Put it there.* Meaning his bad feelings that led to such a situation. Meaning even his dick if that's what he wants. That's fine with me if it doesn't go towards any other unsuspecting subway riders.

But then, just as the train doors are about to close, I see my Goblin again. Her eyes are gleaming red now, she's standing on the platform, her black fur covered in expectant ooze. She roars, *Stop being such a doormat and do it already. On the count of three.*

One

I turn back to him, my face once again screwed into a mask of rage but also something more creative. Something I can one day use to finish this book.

Two

I must look horrifying because he cowers, trying to escape into the dermatology ad behind him. But I won't let him escape. Not this time. This is the last man to show me his rooster and leave unscathed.

Three

My Goblin gives me the signal, and I pull down my pants and show him my Medusa that turns him to stone. I can feel the wind on my snakes. They are more alive than ever, ebullient. They also love the subway. What do I feel in this instant? Every possible thing all at once to the point where it almost unmakes me until I turn it off.

I pull up my pants, gather myself together. I'm happy as hell. Goblin looks like her work here is done. How much of this really happened? You decide. I'll take it to the grave.

As I step off the train, I feel, as my son might say, gobsmacked, but also a little tougher. I look behind me on the platform. My Goblin finally looks so very proud.

59. Wild and Precious Life

After picking up the kids and carting them home, my heart is still pounding from the whole flasher episode, but there's no time to process it, as per usual. The thing is, as a parent I don't have time to be shellshocked. They need me now.

When we get home, my son insists on Bad Bunny, which I can barely listen to anymore, and my daughter requests the Disney Princess Songs on another Spotify account and I toggle between my daughter's and son's different musical-play realities until I feel dizzy and doubled, moving back-and-forth between their clashing dimensions, popping popcorn and striking dramatic poses to "Let it Go" from *Frozen*, taking particular care to belt out the parts about how *the cold never bothered me anyway,* telling the more compelling story of that ice queen before she was defanged, Disneyfied, while nobody listens to me, but I feel better for having provided cultural context, just like in class. I feel a single fang starting to protrude from my gums and I pass my tongue over it with pride.

Then bathing for all. I try to put her in the bath downstairs, ensconced in lavender-scented bubbles, while hoping he's not destroying the upstairs. She clings to me like the world's ending, so I stay until I hear something crash upstairs. Then I rush up to coax him into his shower. I clean up whatever crashed. Then, when he comes out and starts playing Chess Kid while singing "I Want it That Way" for her, finally a bath for me. But not without both kids busting in at different points to take a dump or air grievances as I cower behind the opaque shower curtain. I try to find brain space to think in any sort of creative way or wonder about the significance of life, but mostly just end up drifting through the night in a semi-wakeful state.

I often think of the ending of Mary Oliver's "The Summer Day" and her question of what you are going to do with your *one wild and precious life* as I muddle through my own night in search of meaning. I asked Hector what he thought life was all about and he said coffee, which seemed like a good enough answer to me. Maybe we all tend to think meaning comes from whatever it is we do with our days. I asked my daughter once what the meaning of life was and she said, *Crayola.* I asked my son, and he ignored me because he was playing Minecraft, but it's a form of world-building so I made some allowances for him, as there is meaning to be found there.

I like to put a lot of pressure on my family and place them in uncomfortable ontological positions (just kidding; sort of), so I emailed them the Mary Oliver poem and asked, *what's the meaning of life?*

I figured I wouldn't hear back from anyone, or it would take a long time for the responses to come back, but the answers came pouring in. As you might imagine, I received some lighter and darker responses that reflected the personalities of the responders. My father answered, in his inimitable way, and with a nod to the Oliver poem, *to be one with the grasshopper and the one who made it.*

My mom may not have understood the question, or actually maybe she did. She wrote, *as a child, I lay on the grass watching the clouds and said to myself, 'And I will lie here in my grave forever and ever and ever and ever and ever.* When it comes to the meaning of that one, your guess is as good as mine.

My brother responded with, *my two favorite answers from the pop culture are '42' and 'Life sucks, and then you die.' I don't regard that second one as a joke, I actually think it is a very wise statement. One of my favorite books is* The Plague *by Camus . . . it really encapsulates how I think about the world, and humanity. To the surprise of some people, I consider it to be an optimistic book. Although I'm actually becoming much more cynical these days because of climate change. There we go. Here's an original response: The surface of the planet is now gradually warming to the point where it will likely become uninhabitable, which may well lead to the collapse of civilization within my own lifetime. Why? People are stupid, selfish creatures that are incapable of looking at the long term. So . . . what does that tell you about life? I guess it's not worth very much.*

One of my favorite people in the world, my uncle, who has recently left this world, wrote back something I think of at least once a week: *This time the line that grabbed me was* 'the one who has flung herself out of the grass.' *So, without thinking about it, I will say that the point of life is: while being flung out to consider that—wherever (each time) you land—a lovely poet will receive you, not fling you away in disgust, nor crush you in her palm. And she will feed you sugar.*

60. When We Promise Not to Look

My son's after something similar significance-wise perhaps because we have similar ontological needs when we are early or late in the journey. And then there's the big question. As I put them to bed that night, after *ablutions*, the British sounding, comically formal word for washing up that my mother introduced to them, I sing and do all the occult rituals that enable my children to even attempt to go to bed.

After we have a long conversation about mammals, then one about different kinds of farts, he asks about the meaning of life, like why do we do it? We're not looking each other in the eye when he poses the question, which is what makes it possible. So much finds permission to exist when we promise not to look.

I watched the end of *This is Us* and she's on this train where her kids are at different ages, and in real life they are saying goodbye to her and remembering what a great mom she was. Then she reaches the caboose car and it's time to lie down in this bed. It's comforting and chilling at once, and a pretty accurate rendering of how life and death (probably) feels, given that I know very little of either. But also the episode emphasizes how your kids will remember you, how you shaped them. It reminds me of the question the Fordham student asked me when I gave a talk there recently: *if you don't leave a legacy through children or being a genius, then how do you?* All I could think to share was the legacy of just trying to make the world even infinitesimally better, like go out and paint somebody's fence for them kind of thing. That's as good a legacy as I can imagine. I am trying to focus on building community for others, for my kids, my students, anything to keep my head out of my own behind, as I camp at my desk trying to be Zadie Smith.

61. Surrealist Experiment

After my son's meaning of life question, my daughter can see something crucial is afoot. She decamps from her bed to poke her head into the moment, shoving her face so close our eyes are almost touching. I inevitably become cheered up when she wields her curly mop of a head like a jackhammer. This girl. It's like she popped out of a cartoon or pastoral poem. She looks like Little Bo-Peep and (because my eccentric Mom once inexplicably read her Coleridge to stop her from crying in the car during a rainstorm one time), she sometimes says, *water, water, everywhere* when it rains.

Also, flowers. I've never bought flowers without her tearing them all off to give to people in our building. I'm irritated by the floral defacement but touched by the premise: she doesn't hoard the joy their beauty brings but shares it widely. She doesn't seem quite real, even after all these years of having her live outside my body, in my house. She also makes me laugh so hard. Like that time she begged me to roast imaginary marshmallows for s'mores over the pretend fire she claimed emanated from her ears. I abstained.

But before I could answer my son's question, she loses interest and tries to eat my necklace, saying, *Mommy, back ride.* This is my cue to flip onto my stomach so she can board my back like a sea vessel. I do so. And my son performs his older kid part of the act, just as ardent but at a cooler remove: holding my hand way too tightly and chatting.

My son keeps his distance in a certain way pre-eight p.m., but then he becomes deeply affectionate, and we have long talks every night where he tells me everything that has happened to him since he woke at five. As his hair grazes my cheek and I smell his pine tree smell, every second since he was born tunnels back to me, and I feel the electric currents of his mind coursing through my own neural pathways. (Please don't edit me for science.) I kiss his forehead and think on that moment of Dr. Frankenstein giving life to his creature with all the lightning in the movie version. Sometimes I have the sick thought that I could never write anything better than my kids, so why even try. They are texturally layered in a way that would be hard to do with a book.

But I must also pursue my written structures. It's hard to explain to people who don't feel this way, but I don't have a choice. It's a passion but, let's be honest, it's also a compulsion for which one requires Dr. Frankenstein's *workshop of filthy creation*—part of why I understand the iconography of the Frankenstein movie lightning creation moment as not only campily over-the-top but also just the right level of peak drama. My professor friend of the fries and good diner coffee recently gave me a Frankenstein T-shirt and I vowed to never take it off, especially since I seem to be incapable of writing a book that doesn't reference the book or movie.

My son, too, is obsessed with structures. Sometimes I picture his understanding of the world like how the child protagonist of *Queen's Gambit* sees chess games on her ceiling at night. We travel on the weekends for his tournaments, and he plays with whoever will respond to his portable chess board at the local playground or in Union Square Park, where grown men with cigarettes dangling from their mouths try to wipe the floor with my son while crowds capture it on their iPhones. He once explained to me how he imagines whatever is happening before him in the world as having a parallel or shadow existence in his mind as he receives it (not how he put it but still), and it was like he was narrating how I think back to me through a megaphone, and I felt so understood. Then he asked if he could go back to playing videogames.

During this peculiar nocturnal ritual, I pause—then and only then—the infinite march of my thoughts. Some ideas are zombified, charging onward aimlessly, while others sharpen the brain substance. This bedtime ritual removes all thoughts entirely, leaving my head shiny and new. The only other way to achieve this sort of ecstatic mental emptiness is staring at the wall or sitting in my parents' yard with the turkeys.

The surrealist experiment of putting the kids to bed is an anomaly in which time, space, and technology cease. I rarely bring my phone because I want this child land to remain pure of the electromagnetic nightmare field of my email inbox for one thing. This morning there was an *SOS* at the top of my iPhone, as though I needed any more symbology of technological apocalypse. And so, there's really something to not letting that electronic fount of longing and aspiration anywhere near the numinous child's kingdom of their room, characterized as it is by the strange whirr of the probably haunted furnace, perennial smell of juice, and sting of Legos underfoot.

62. A Poltergeist Situation

Their rooms are now on the bottom floor, which wasn't easy since there are strange noises that I believe emanate from the furnace (?) but also maybe it's a Poltergeist situation. At one point, after a picture fell from the wall while we were discussing it, my daughter named the spirit to make it less scary. So, don't worry about that eerie rumbling over there; that's just Gumby. Kidding. Mostly. Sometimes I wonder if it's Goblin, and what my kids would think of her. I picture them playing a huge game of Twister in the basement, their limbs becoming indecipherable. I would join in, braid all our thoughts together to read in the future and call it memory.

I can barely breathe with my daughter on top of me. My face is comically smashed to the side to the point where I wonder if it could possibly come off or stay that way. Both my stomach and what I can only call my capacity for closeness are being pushed to the limit as usual. I picture it in a way that's Seussical. I see the coiling and bizarre labyrinth of my love being forced by these strange beings to stretch and rise, and rise and stretch, until it's so overdrawn it looks like it might tear in half. But it never does.

But to bring it back to the philosophical matter at hand, I say to my son: *Remember how you asked why we do it?* Of course, he doesn't, even though it was mere minutes ago, and says, *nope.* Even the most important thoughts drift away from these kids so suddenly. I say, *you asked me why we do all the stuff. I think our nights have something to do with it.*

My daughter wants to be part of the conversation but doesn't understand it, so she repeats my last words in a thoughtful tone, as she often does: *do with it.*

Then, he says, *yeah, what's the point if we all die in the end?*

My daughter says: *die in the end*, and I see that I'll have to bring out the heavy metaphysical equipment tonight.

He wants to know where he will go, and where my father will go, and whether it will be a nice place. I feel the answer must be yes, and so I give it, because I'm not so sure that saying we all might just fade into the earth will really be any comfort to my children.

At the onset of COVID, my kids became afraid at bedtime again. They were no longer scared of Gumby, and it wasn't even monsters anymore, but rather other unknown forces that do in fact eventually take us. Supernatural horror is just a filing cabinet for the very real terrors of being alive, such as suffering, or the flashing end of this life ahead of us all.

My kids were living through a plague, after all. They didn't want to go to sleep because they didn't want to die. I was faced with the awkwardness of being someone with no religious affiliation trying to comfort them, and therefore telling them about something like heaven, that nobody knows what happens when we die, but some people do think we go to a wonderful place. *Is there even cherry Jell-O? Yes, even cherry Jell-O.* The act of imagining for them this space was another way of writing, but writing with them as protagonists—their wonderful wouldn't be my wonderful, so how to imagine myself into their imaginations? It was another form of time and space travel in the name of love.

63. Monstrous Hell-Bride

It hurts to have my son squeezing my hand and my daughter on my back, but there's also some meaning of life to be found in their nightly demonstrations of outlandish tenderness. I picture my daughter ferreting me off on a "back ride" whenever I want to run away. I'd start a nice life by the sea, somewhere far from technology, bikini waxes and PTA meetings, where I could write in peace or even just go to the bathroom without small people busting in to touch me with ketchup fingers while singing songs they learned from animated beings.

The whole bizarre premise of our bedtime routine is probably the meaning of life my son is asking about, or one of them. But writing is also part of it for me. How to articulate this to them? I finally say, *I think the point of life is what you love, like I love both of you and I also love my writing.* Silence.

And then he says, *oh, like how I love you but also chess? Absolutely.* My daughter adds, *and crayons*, and we nod sagely because we do, in fact, get what she's saying. So maybe she understood all along.

When I mentally drift off during our bedtime routine, I remind myself, as my son always says, to *soak it all in.* I remember that soon, way sooner than I'd like, they won't beg to lie on my back at night, or ask to be "haired," which involves cascading my very long hair around their little thrilled faces and drawing it slowly from forehead to chin until they howl with delight. The salty Play-Doh smell of their skin, the tickle of her curly hair on my shoulders, his hard hugs that take the wind from me, his "final cuddle" in which my daughter and I pretend, gently, to fight over him, and how he savors it, as I whisk myself out of the nightly brain-death of Netflix and sugar binge. We throw our whole bodies at my son who wrestles with us and hugs back so tightly I literally have bruises from loving him. But, see, this is it. This is the whole thing. Also Goblin mode.

64. Tundras of Domesticity

As I pass the full-length mirror after escaping their room, I glimpse something monstrous that turns out to be just me without my glasses. Yet I feel I've seen my own potential creative ferocity beckoning to me from the shores of creative lands I can't reach with two children on my back. Or can I? But how?

As Virginia Woolf's "a room of one's own" simply isn't possible for me, the only solution I have found is to include my kids in my creative life. Even if that means attempting to type with both on my lap smearing my keys with what I can only hope is chocolate. A different kind of writer's block: I spend most of my writing time trying to peer over one or both of their heads, to reach the keys as they sit on my lap. They've already come upstairs. They're here now. They always are. Often they read what I'm writing, so I have to be careful. They just caught me writing about them. They want me to tell you they say *hi*.

The underlying message of modern motherhood: don't stress but work one hundred hours a week and be home in time to make homemade organic baby food in an ancient butter churner while looking stunning and ensuring your kids can speak to fairies and save the world. This is not tenable. Because what happens if you worked a hundred hours and then your kid doesn't want to talk to fairies or eat organic baby food made in the ancient butter churner? You get furious is what happens. Not fun for any party involved.

Over the years, there have been countless essays about the monstrosity of mothers taking time to write, and how this might turn them into Grendel's mother, storming up with their son's claw in hand and kidnapping one of the Scyldings from the mead-hall. But I'm not too worried about this. Frankly, in my perennial professor-and-mother role as kindly, caretaking older lady, I'm not really in danger of becoming a monstrous hell-bride. What feels villainous to me, however, is any behavior that isn't selfless, such as getting a babysitter to take my kids to the mind-numbing kid sing-along in my stead so I can blast metal, pound energy drinks, be the werewolf roaming my own wilderness long enough to finally attempt to finish this book, which I've started in fits and starts, on scraps of paper, in various technological formats, in my daughter's bathtub crayons, on the dusty subway windows, in its snaking tunnels in graffiti, in sky writing, on the walls of my college's bathrooms, and on the back of your hand with a Bic pen. Hell, I'd write it in blood if it came to it and you know it.

I will never forget the day my kids came to see me read for the first time. I have a picture of the instant these two theoretically irreconcilable worlds touched. There I was: reading about stalking my own creativity through tundras of domesticity; and there were my kids: the central inhabitant of these tundras, sitting crisscross-applesauce in the front row. It seemed to blow their little minds that I existed as something other than a humanoid teat, but this discovery of who I was in my entirety turned out to be important for all of us.

After the reading, my son had many questions. *Was I a famous writer,* for instance? *Um…no, not at all.* And, from that night on, after any intense experience, he'd ask me whether I was going to write about it. *Um…absolutely.* He started discussing this book-in-progress with me. As I was writing, he'd place his little notebook across from mine so we could write together like some old-timey screenwriting duo: me on this and he on his (admittedly shorter but no less serious, let me tell you) stories for school.

He wrote one called, *SNAKES!* that had both a table of contents and a glossary. He'd ask me what "my story" was about and I'd do the same until our narratives started speaking to each other from across the table, becoming braided narratives, which is also of course how I made my children in the first place. What could be more of a braided narrative than baby making? Most of all, he likes to help me with edits. I run things by him. In fact, he weighed in on the other potential title for this book, swiftly nixing it with an opinionated *nuh-uh,* because it *had too many words and you shouldn't use Mr. Potato Head in a title.* And who can argue with that?

65. Underground Creature of Joy

Of course, I couldn't answer my son's question about the meaning of life in any definitive way, but I can tell you a story that gestures towards a kind of answer. After I finally coax them to bed again, my daughter has a nightmare and comes upstairs. I'm now sitting here watching her draw and eat green beans.

As she sets down a green bean to concentrate on the drawing, she stares back at me with these over-the-top-observant blue eyes with highly curled lashes, looking at me like she knows everything already. She's like the original Emerson-style poet, listening to the music of the universe as it comes over the transom. Maybe one day she will tell me what she hears. I write this as I look at her. She knows I'm writing about her and says, *make me a green unicorn in your book, mama.* And I say, *okay, but you make me one, too.* She nods, stuffing another bean into her mouth.

She navigates this world of our apartment like a drunken sailor, bopping up against the veil between the different worlds of the ornate toy assemblages she creates when I'm not looking. I step in patches of paint every time I go to the bathroom at night, and I experience an amalgam of rage and affection every time I do so. She also turns all the food I give her into art scenes, sculpturally shaping even green beans into unexpected forms. She likes most of all to pause between the before and the after, just marveling, as I do. Before, it's a green bean, but after? It's art. That's the transformation.

More specifically, initially it's a green bean but then it's a green fragmented unicorn on my kitchen table. It's an irritating habit, my house is never clean, I must lecture her on not doing this at other people's houses, but most of me is exhilarated by this little creative child art anarchist who lives with me and turns even this mediocre green bean casserole into art.

66. Green Fragmented Unicorn

I know how it will turn out, so I save time. I carefully tear the green beans into little pieces and pass them over to her on the wood table. At first, she surprises me, as she always does, by eating some, in great big scoops. Then, as I know she will, she builds her structures. Strange bean warrens suddenly showing up on my table after I come back from getting the laundry. Green fragmented unicorns.

Now, as I fold the laundry, she's leaning her head on my shoulder, and I'm thinking about how all I do now is hold on to her, hold on and hold on. But I'm also thinking how one day she'll learn to ride a bike, go on a date, go to college. I'll run behind her and behind her—and then one day I'll let go. I know it should be "beautiful," but I quickly eat a bunch of green beans to keep from sobbing because I'm not ready to let go. But I must. That's another unthinkable impossibility I live with daily. But I guess there was a time when I couldn't imagine her living outside of me, and here we are, so I suppose it's all a process.

I want to stop time so I can stay in this green bean place with her, writing stories only about green beans on typewriters made of green beans. But, instead, I walk her back down to bed and we make walrus sounds until she finally crashes back into sleep. I watch her sleeping face like it has something to tell me.

After I've put her back to bed, I fall asleep at the table, drooling on my magnum opus. I wake up to discover all I have written is "Magnum Opus."

And now I see my son peering at me. Wonder how long he's been awake and what he's been doing all this time. Not let myself think about it. Notice that he's taken the green beans and is starting to position them on his chessboard and asking if I want to play green bean chess. When will this day ever end? Will it ever end?

I start to lose my patience. He rushes into the other room for a second. I wonder if I looked that angry. But when he comes back, he's holding something. He says, *you need your thinking cap*. He gives me a hat that resembles a gigantic blueberry, *a thinking cap to help me think of good writing*. He'd made it in school. I put on my new cap, remember why I do any of it, tell myself if I never write anything worthwhile, at least I have the braided narrative of these loopy, never-ending days with my kids.

I put him back to bed, before the next day inevitably starts when tiny sticky fingers brush my face as I feel my daughter sitting on my head while her brother screams from the other room that his head is stuck in the laundry basket again. I still feel surrounded by death and destruction but there's something else: some underground creature of joy poking its head out of the ground.

Goblin comes to stand behind me as I pull the patched chair up to this computer yet again. But this time, I'm not blocked. I feel storm patterns inside that indicate the rest of the writing's finally coming. Rough patches of words. Slashes of image threatening to tear open my inner systems. Before it goes away, I shove green beans in my mouth, and start typing so that one day I can read my own name on the surface of ghosts.

Acknowledgments

Thanks to the *Kenyon Review*, the *Pine Hills Review*, *Elle*, and *Electric Lit* for publishing earlier versions of sections of this book. I am deeply grateful to Andrew Gifford, Susan Schulman, and the Santa Fe Writers Project team for their work on this book and belief in me.

While writing this book, I relied on the support of the long-suffering love of my life, Adriel Gerard, whose privacy I have tried to respect in this work, but who hides behind every page of this book.

This book wouldn't exist without Max and Layla, who asked to be part of this project. I have honored this request, just in a speculative way that includes lots of things that aren't actually true about them or the world we live in together. I think they will enjoy this, and I hope they won't hate it when they're older.

And how could I forget my parents, Trish and Louis Hagood, who called me a writer from a young age?

I also couldn't have written this book without my students.

I am grateful to the family, colleagues, and friends who have supported me by reading early versions of this work, coming to my readings, and generally supporting my writing life over the years: Judi Weinstock, Charley Gerard, Eva Gerard, Phil Bender, Kay Whitney, Sherry Frazer, Phil Gerard, Natalie Hennessy, Heidi Bender, Mike Bender, Sue Gussow, Mimi Nelson, Miku Terai, Daniella Furman, Julie Mulligan, Julia Goldstein, Emily Bona-Cohen, Adrianne Fiala, Jill DiDonato, Sophie Roberts, Dana Reichman, Jeanne Puchir, Kristen Puchir, Robert Puchir, Bret Puchir, Nishi Shah, Wendy Chin-Tanner, Joanna Fuhrman, Jiwon Choi, Mark Pawlak, Bob Hershon, Elizabeth Hershon, Donna Hershon Keri Smith, Dick Lourie, Patricia Grisafi, Cristina Baptista, Amie Souza Reilly, Leonard Cassuto, Heather Dubrow, Sarah Gambito, Elisabeth Frost, Melissa Ostrom, Amy Lorraine Long, Kayla Webley, Ben Adler, Jerry Adler, Beth Lebowitz, Anna Beskin, Jane van Slembrouck, Sharon Mesmer, David

Coates, Rebecca Lehde, Jahnvi Shah, Sagar Shah, Sam Levy, Carol Levy, Matthew Daddona, Seb Doubinsky, Robert P. Ottone, Nicholas Birns, Margaret Boe Birns, Marty Skoble, Veronica Russo, Linda Greenberg, Marc Vincenz, T. Thilleman, Al Zuckerman, Jennifer Ryan, Barish Ali, Peter Ramos, Karen Sands-O'Connor, Aimable Twagilimana, Diane Kistner, Joan Erskine, Sofia Zambenedetti, Ariel Zambenedetti, Josephine Kuhl, Theo Gangi, Ghazala Afzal, Ian Maloney, Jason Dubow, Emily Edwards, Jen Wingate, Athena Devlin, Jive Poetic, Virginia Franklin, Gregory Tague and Mitch Levenberg—my professor friend of the fries and good diner coffee (without whose help I would definitely not have this job I love).

About the Author

PHOTO: Alice Teeple

Caroline Hagood is an Assistant Professor of Literature, Writing and Publishing and Director of Undergraduate Writing at St. Francis College in Brooklyn, where she also teaches in the creative writing MFA program. She is the author of two poetry books; the essay collections, *Ways of Looking at a Woman and Weird Girls: Writing the Art Monster*; and the novels, *Ghosts of America* and *Filthy Creation*. Her work has appeared in publications including *Electric Literature, Creative Nonfiction, LitHub, the Kenyon Review, the Huffington Post, the Guardian, Salon*, and *Elle*. She lives in Brooklyn with her family and spends most of her time trying to get them to read weird books. Find her at carolinehagood.com

Also from Santa Fe Writers Project

Magic For Unlucky Girls *by A.A. Balaskovits*

The fourteen fantastical stories in *Magic For Unlucky Girls* take the familiar tropes of fairy tales and twist them into new and surprising shapes. These unlucky girls, struggling against a society that all too often oppresses them, are forced to navigate strange worlds as they try to survive.

> *"A wonderful, truly original work."*
> —Emily St. John Mandel, author of Station Eleven

Modern Manners for Your Inner Demons
by Tara Laskowski

Laskowski's demonically clever stories break the rules of a "decent" society, providing a definitive guide on the etiquette of obesity, dementia, infertility, homicide, arson, and more.

Strange Folk You'll Never Meet
by A.A. Balaskovits

With elements of psychological horror, sly humor, and the fantastic, these stories will burrow under your skin, haunt your dreams, and make you wonder what worlds lie just beyond that tiny hole in the wall.

About Santa Fe Writers Project

SFWP is an independent press founded in 1998 that embraces a mission of artistic preservation, recognizing exciting new authors, and bringing out of print work back to the shelves.

  @santafewritersproject | @SFWP | sfwp.com